Billy Cowie

Silent Land

Published 2017
by idiolect,
92 Centurion Road,
Brighton,
East Sussex,
BN1 3LN
(Kindle Edition 2012)

cover painting Silke Mansholt
Printed and bound in Great Britain by TJ International Ltd, Padstow

ISBN-13 978-0-9554004-3-8
ISBN-10 0-9554004-3-0

for Silke

I have been here before,
But when or how I cannot tell:
I know the grass beyond the door,
The sweet keen smell,
The sighing sound, the lights around the shore.

Dante Gabriel Rossetti 'Sudden Light'

PROLOGUE

You are already familiar with the room – you have seen its copies hundreds of times in films and TV shows – though usually it is better lit than it is today, the highlights just so, the shadows carefully placed. In fact the first thing its ever so slightly disappointed new owner always says is, 'hey, pretty stuffy with that new carpet smell and everything in here; let's get some light in, draw the curtains, open the windows up.' Though usually after a few months they are happy to let as little light in as possible.

The current occupant is sitting at his desk; he has a number but I don't recall it. They always have numbers these guys (and they're nearly always guys), a bit like convicts, though the numbers are shorter as there aren't as many of them and of course fewer of them are innocent. He is watching his clock as it approaches 9. He follows the second hand as it sweeps up to the top of the dial and he silently counts down. Right on the button he hears a familiar voice.

'Knock knock, Mr President, you got time for something bizarre and unusual?' Joel does his comedy knock on the imaginary closed door and enters smiling.

'Joel, come on in, always got time for the bizarre and unusual.'

The President leans to his intercom,

'Helen, sweetie? Can you hold the mundane and normal for twenty minutes?'

The answer is shouted from the next room – she can never be bothered to lean over and push that little button,

'You got it, Pres.'

The President sucks in his top lip momentarily,

'Tell me, Joel, do you think her attitude is just a little informal?'

Joel puts the pile of papers, with two neighbourhood deli coffees balanced on the top, carefully on the desk.

'Whatever gets you through the day, sir.'

The President picks up one of the two cardboard cups.

'You'd think that the leader of the most powerful nation in the world could get some decent coffee in his own place,' he says, as he always does.

Actually he can get better coffee here, much better, but truth be told he likes the little rituals and this is one of his favourites.

'So sit down, Joel. Spill the bizarre beans.'

Joel sits on the corner of the desk and takes his time with his answer.

'Man walks into a private investigator's office in LA.'

'I'm taking it that the PI was one of our guys?'

'Of course. The fellow has this bundle of info about some Mexican he wanted checking out. Our man figures he can make it a little Mexican vacation so heads down there and checks out the details.' He hands the President some sheets, 'These are copies of what he came up with; the stuff ringed in red was correct, the stuff in blue was way wrong and the stuff in green he couldn't find out.'

The President flicks through the pages.

'I don't see any blue.'

'There isn't any; everything he managed to check out was correct, even the tiniest details.'

The President throws the papers casually back onto the desk,

'So what?'

'Point is this guy lived a hundred years ago.'

'So double what?'

'Our guy comes back, delivers his report, thinks he might as well check out the guy who did the asking and follows him.'

'So who was he?'

'The name's Liddell, English scientist, works for some institution called KARC.'

The President puts his hands behind his head and leans back,

'The Klein Amnesia Research Centre?'

Joel fails to hide his surprise at the erudition of his boss – much to the President's pleasure,

'You see, Joel, I do read some of those godawful reports you pile on top of me once in a while. But remind me just what the hell they're doing up there, some memory stuff?'

'Place was set up around a year ago by Joe Klein in the

Santa Monica Mountains. His son, Joe Junior, was in an accident, auto I think, lost a huge part of his memory. Daddy wanted him to get it back.'

'Didn't they bring over some French wunderkind to head it up – Robespierre was it?'

'Close but no cigar, sir. It was a certain Professor Richelieu actually. They have about ten patients at the moment, if that, including Joe Klein Junior, all with post traumatic amnesia. Richelieu brought over Liddell as his assistant from England. Before that he, Liddell that is, was working on prions.'

'The mad cow things?'

'Now you are just bragging, Mr President, Sir.'

The President smiles and takes a sip of his coffee. Still too hot, he puts the cup back down.

'Well Joel, to be frank, I am just a little disappointed in this story. Could been one of their patients remembered something their Mexican grand pappy told him and they wanted to check it out. Who knows or cares? Why are you so fascinated, and what do you suggest we do about it?'

'Well, they have no Mexican patients for a start. I think a little digging is called for. I never liked that Klein family in the first place. Let's send someone in as a patient.'

'You have someone in mind?'

'I was thinking of one of the agents from the Carlson Oil fiasco.'

The President closes his eyes,

'Don't remind me. Didn't fifteen of our people get killed when it got screwed up? My first months in office too.'

'Exactly. That's why the only survivor, our agent, has a big chunk of memory missing.'

'I'd rather send in somebody healthy, even to something

as trivial as this.'

'Problem is they have a scanner they use on new patients. A non-amnesiac would show up.'

'OK, OK. What's his name?' The President is already bored with this story and his mind has moved on. Joel however is looking strangely thoughtful,

'Her name, sir. It's Costello.'

SANTA MONICA

Costello has been heading down Route 101; it is early in the morning and the traffic is light. She puts her arm out the open window and onto the roof in the breeze. She really hates it when guys do that but thinks it is probably all right for her. There are two distinct notes in the noise from the Mustang's engine and Costello sometimes sings a third to complete the chord. Not today the minor note; no, today is a good day and we will have the major note, but just to tease it she suspends it as a fourth before letting it fall. She has been feeling altogether lighter since three days ago when she got the call from Joel and the promise of her first real job since the accident. For one and a half years she has been an errand boy.

Like everyone else she can't quite pin down her feelings for Joel. Sure he looked after her following the accident, put her back on her feet, visited her in hospital. At first she thought he was coming on to her and was annoyed; then when nothing happened between them she was also annoyed – she even wondered if he was gay. Now her theory is that he is somehow asexual. But whatever her feelings for him that phone call from him had gotten her out of the bureau filing office where she had been endlessly sifting records. Two days of intensive background building had followed where she had been allowed to participate fully – always keeping in mind that the best cover is closest to the truth. Never invent when you can bend. They had decided to keep in the oil platform, the explosions, the deaths of her co-workers and leave out only who they had all been working for. This altered version of her life was as tight as a drum, why she even believed some of it herself.

She had been on the 101 all the way from San Francisco but turned off at Oxnard to join the Pacific Coast Highway and spend the last of her drive by the sea. She is puzzled by her mission; why is it taking place at all? A couple of European doctors running a clinic, fair enough there seems to be plenty of money around, but then there must be hundreds of clinics around LA, most of them with some very interesting clientele.

She pulls off the highway at Paradise Cove and drives down to the familiar restaurant. The place is deserted; she parks at the back of the bar which looks like it hasn't changed in the nearly thirty years since she last saw it, walks down to the sea, which is pretty far in, and turns right up the coast. She takes off her sneakers, stuffs her socks in them, puts them round her neck and gingerly paddles round the cliff. Hopefully the tide is going out otherwise she might end up having to be rescued by the coast guard – not a good start to her new mission. The beach is completely empty and she sits on a rock facing the sea. For the first time in twelve months she tries looking into the black hole in her memory that is the incident. On one side there are the preparations, crystal clear, and on the other her time in the military hospital, also firmly etched. Then fringing into the middle space is the information she was told about what happened, sketchy and not real, definitely not connected to her. Maybe these guys at this clinic she is headed for really know what they are doing and can shine some light into that void. Like her prototype hero (or is it heroine? no hero will do, like actor, not actress) would decide, some energetic exercise will help. She puts just the sneakers back on; they need a wash, and jogs through the shallow waves up the coast all the way to the steep cliff steps. These she takes two at a time rocketing her heartbeat, right up to the top of Point Dume where she has to bend double to catch her breath.

She looks down at a far below rock in the sea. She shuts one eye and then moves her head till the blind spot where her optic nerve enters the back of her eye hits the rock and it disappears, washed in by her brain with sea to fill the gap – just like her brain fills in that memory-challenged week. Who was that English king who used to place the blind spot on his courtiers heads to see what they would look like after he beheaded them?

When she gets back to the restaurant it is still closed. Some young guy is moving some deep freeze boxes round to the back.

'Any chance of a coffee?'

'We're closed.'

'Pleeease?'

When Costello does her long pleeease she usually gets

what she wants and this is no exception. The young guy even joins her with a cup himself and waves away her offer of payment,

'Where are you headed?'

'Up to the clinic.'

'Which one?'

'I forget.'

'Oh, sure, that one.'

'You know it?'

'Yeh, they are always coming down here, pretty lively bunch. Happy bunnies you could say.'

'French guy with them?'

'Nope, know who you mean, never seen him, some English doctor is always in charge.'

'Liddell?'

'Yep, could be that name. Why're you going there?'

'I forget.'

He rubs his brow,

'They do all that stuff too. Can get a bit wearisome after a while.'

'Sorry. Yeh I had some memory problems; might check in and see if they can do anything for me.'

Costello turns her red 66 Mustang into the drive of the Centre, still exhilarated by driving up the steep and wildly twisting canyon road at just slightly above a safe speed. She has tuned the engine herself and always feels it is wasted just cruising down a straight highway.

The building is very modern – lots of glass and steel all at strange angles. Doors are open so she wanders in.

'Anybody home?' she calls out. No reply.

She walks down a corridor, and sees a woman reading a book, sitting on a narrow window ledge.

'Professor Richelieu?'

'Not me, honey,' the woman answers without looking up.

'No, I mean is he around?'

The woman folds the corner of her page, closes the book and looks Costello up and down.

'We call him Richy, and he is everywhere. He pervades the building, everything we do. He is here, there and everywhere. He is our guru,' she makes some kind of yoga position with her hands on this last line.

'I was meaning more of a corporeal presence, prick me do I not bleed kind of thing?'

'I see where you're coming from, his body you mean. Yep, his body is probably in his office as we speak. You a new patient?'

'Possibly, is it a good place to come?'

'Does what it says on the tin.'

'Which is?'

'*Mem'ries,*

Light the corners of my mind,

Misty water-coloured memories

Of the way we were,' she sings in a warbling Streisand impression.

The visitor extends a hand,

'I'm Costello.'

The woman takes her hand with a little bow.

'I'm…I'm mmm… oh…'

Seeing the worried look on Costello's face the woman smiles.

'Just my little joke, we do that stuff all the time around here, I'm Maybel. You just go right on past the swimming pool and then on the left you'll see a room full of computers, next to that is his office. He's always in there.'

Costello sets off down the corridor,

'Catch you later.'

Maybel goes back to her book and her Streisand song.

'Mem'ries, may be beautiful and yet
What's too painful to remember
We simply choose to forget.'

Costello winces and turns back to her,

'Hey, don't give up your day job, Maybel.'

She goes on past a swimming pool with a couple of people in it and then as Maybel had said a room with lots of computers with a solitary guy in the middle. Then a couple of offices. The door of one is slightly open; she knocks and pushes it a little further ajar,

'Professor Richelieu?'

He stands up,

'Ms Costello, I presume, pleasant trip?'

Costello had built up a mental picture of the professor to resemble the little drug runner in *The French Connection*, the one with the small grey beard, but Richelieu is quite tall and more like the Gene Hackman character, what's his name, Popeye or something?

(ALTMAN 253: look not at the photograph of those you are going to meet, you know them not, why should you know them?)

'Not bad, traffic was light. Nice place you got here. Is that for real?' she gestures at the large Degas painting behind the professor.

'Absolutely, you may also see a Kandinsky and a few Monets around. My personal favourites are the Corots actually.'

'And there is no security, I mean at the front? I just walked right in.'

'If the price of having the paintings was having some asshole with a gun running around then I would have happily have had them put in the bank.'

'Nice to be relaxed about it, must be worth something, this whole place and all. It's pretty big.'

'Thanks to the kind beneficence of Mr. Klein we lack for nothing. No expenses spared.'

'His son is here, isn't he?'

'Young Joe, yes, our first patient in fact.'

'How's he doing?'

'Strictly speaking I shouldn't discuss another patient but you will see him around, and I think you will agree, just fine. He could leave really but apparently he likes it here, made quite a few friends.'

'You can't exactly kick him out can you?'

'We wouldn't want to, but his father is so pleased with his progress we could do or ask for anything we wanted.'

Richelieu sounds determined to suppress his French accent but it is leaking out despite his efforts.

(ALTMAN 22: say something stupid, the stupid are beyond suspicion.)

'Do you have any monkeys around?'

'Monkeys? Ah Ms Costello, you are testeenng ma acsont, non?' Richelieu goes totally *Pink Panther* Clouseau for the line and they both laugh.

'But to business. Let me just find out where my colleague

Liddell is?' Richelieu opens up his computer and sends a quick email and a few minutes later gets a reply.

'He will be with us in a half hour. Perhaps you would like to take some breakfast on the patio. Anton, our beloved cook, will get you whatever you want and we will join you when Liddell arrives. Down the corridor and through the French windows at the end.'

Costello gives him a little wave and goes through the doors. Despite having seen some pretty spectacular views on her way up she is completely taken aback by the sight of the valley. The building appears to have been unnaturally extended out so that it feels as if you are floating in space. Costello gingerly tests the security of the metal railing that fills the little gaps in the stone wall round the edge of the terrace; it feels pretty strong but she still chooses a seat a little way away from the edge. She has this thing since she was a child, the idea that in two seconds of madness she might just throw herself over; she gets it bad in theatres where the seats are steeply raked. Strangely in enclosed spaces she is totally happy with heights, even been known to lie flat spread-eagled on the glass floor of the Toronto CN Tower trying to persuade her then boyfriend to take a photo, him being too scared to even get close.

'Hi.'

Costello jumps as she is pulled back out of her reverie by a blonde guy wearing a large black apron.

'Sorry, I didn't mean to startle you. I'm Anton.'

They shake hands.

'What would you like for breakfast?'

'What have you got?'

'Everything.'

Unlike Richelieu Anton makes not the slightest effort to disguise his French accent.

'Oh no, too much choice, you tell me.'

Anton looks her up and down, tilts his head to the side and hmms a bit. Then nods sagely,

'Scrambled eggs on toast with black coffee?'

'Perfect.'

Anton goes and Costello picks up a paper lying on the table.

He returns in five minutes with a little tray with the coffee and eggs.

He waits as Costello picks up her fork. She puts some egg in her mouth and then closes her eyes.

'I'm getting something a little strange here?'

'Cinnamon.'

Costello opens her eyes and gets down on one knee,

'Anton, will you marry me?'

'I'm afraid there is unfortunately already a small queue ahead of you.'

'Put me in that line.'

She tests the coffee.

'Happy days are here again.'

Anton gives a little nod and then disappears.

Costello savours her breakfast. A small bird pops up on the railing. A delicate grey and brown with beautiful circles round its eyes. Costello tosses it a few crumbs and it hops onto the table.

'Spiels breweri breweri.'

'Pardon?'

'Commonly known as Brewster's Sparrow. I'm Doctor Liddell, I take it you are Ms Costello?'

'Just Costello.'

Liddell sits down next to her. Once again Costello had built up a mental image in advance that was somewhere between Hugh Grant and John Lennon but Liddell if anything looks rather Italian.

He is carrying a file that must be about her.

Richelieu strolls onto the patio.

'Everything fine with the breakfast?' he asks rhetorically, 'I see you two have met.'

'Doctor Liddell was just introducing me to our little buddy here.' The sparrow is unperturbed by the new arrivals and searches out the last of the crumbs.

Richelieu makes a face,

'Please don't encourage him, he'll end up telling you what their favourite insect is and what colour their droppings are and...'

Luckily Anton arrives back with a cappuccino he puts down before Liddell and an espresso with an almond croissant he puts in front of Richelieu.

'Nice view you got here. Where's Los Angeles?' Costello asks.

'Behind that conveniently placed mountain, thank goodness,' Liddell answers her.

'Isn't there some painter that paints this valley stuff? I've seen some exhibition in San Francisco.'

Richelieu answers,

'You mean Hockney, the Englishman. I think he lived somewhere in this very valley. There is some story he turned up at Klein's door when Klein was still living here. Wanted to paint this exact view. Klein even bought the picture; it's in one of the bedrooms.'

'Sounds like you don't like it too much?'

'The painting is all right, a bit garish for my taste, but the painter is a stupid old fool, always banging on about his right to smoke everywhere. Just because he's survived doesn't give him the right to condemn other people to an early death.'

'In fact,' Liddell joins in, 'that's the whole problem. Kids hear that smoking takes five years off your life and think, hey I live eighty or seventy-five years what's the difference? Those last ones are pretty crap years anyway; what they don't realise is, it is an average of five years. For some, like that painter guy, it makes no difference but then others die in their forties. Which are not crap years.'

Costello puts her hands up to stem the tirade,

'Hold on guys. Sounds like a pretty hot topic for you two.'

'Well if you try sitting across from a mother with two little children on her knee trying to think of some way of telling her she is not going to see them get to secondary school, it might be a hot topic for you too.'

'Fair enough. I'm clean by the way, haven't touched one for ten years. Honest to God.'

'I'm glad to hear it.'

Richelieu looks at the file he has taken from Liddell,

'Maria Costello?'

'Just Costello, please.'

'Thirty-two years old. You had an accident not quite two years ago. Can you tell us about it in your own words?'

'Do you want to know what I can actually remember or what has been pieced together by other people and told to me?'

'Both would be useful.'

‘OK, I was at the time working for OHSD, that is the Occupation Health and Safety Department, as an inspector. I specialised in marine environments, mostly ships, dockyards. Two weeks before the accident things start to get hazy. I do remember inspecting a large naval vessel. After that we are in the realms of speculation. Apparently I had an assignment to check over an off shore oilrig in the Caribbean. Pretty routine stuff. The head technician had arranged to meet me from the helicopter to plan out the visit. Apparently shortly after my arrival the whole rig erupted. I was picked up from the sea with pretty bad burns, the only survivor. I was in some hospital when I woke up.’

‘How long would you say the gap is in your memory?’ Liddell asks. Costello notes he has a light moustache from his cappuccino froth.

‘It’s about three or four weeks depending on how you count the hazy. Let’s say three weeks of absolute zero.’

Richelieu takes over the questioning again, making quick notes in her file,

‘Were you unconscious for most of that period?’

‘Apparently not. I was only out for six or seven hours. But the early hospital stuff I don’t remember either.’

‘Do you have any other memories that have been affected by the incident?’

‘How would I know about them?’

‘For example recollections of colleagues involved or maybe killed quite often become a little blurry.’

‘I didn’t know anyone else involved,’ Costello lies. In reality five of her closest friends from the service were with her and she can only remember their names by a series of mnemonics one of the rehab psychologists had taught her.

'Well nothing you have told us sounds too serious and that raises the first question we must ask you: why do you wish to retrieve these memories? Why not let sleeping dogs lie? Just get on with your life. The amnesia does not seem to be affecting you adversely.'

'Aren't you doing yourself out of a job?'

'Our prime goal is your wellbeing, Ms Costello, and if that means doing nothing then we are only too happy to do it.'

'Well, there are a couple of insurance issues that I'd like to get sorted out but my main aim is to recover a bit of myself. I just want to know what happened to me.'

Liddell takes back over,

'So, first we will need to do a scan of your brain to see if we can help.'

'What sort of scan?'

'An MRI, only fifteen minutes.'

'Is that one of those long tube things? I get a touch claustrophobic.'

'No it's just a short tube and most of your body remains outside. It's called a short bore MRI. Most patients don't have any problems with it. We can do it straight away, if you are finished your breakfast? The scan room is at the other end of the corridor where you came in.'

Costello reluctantly puts down her fork,

'Lets go.'

She walks with them back up through the long corridor. The place is massive with spectacular views on every side. At the scan room Liddell hands her over to a nurse.

Liddell and Richelieu go into the control room. Liddell closes the door softly,

'Well, I told you she was suspicious.'

'Merde. I thought we would have longer. What do you think, FBI?'

'Who knows, maybe CIA or even an agency we never even heard of. I knew that guy in LA was trouble; I should have gone to Mexico myself.'

'Spilt milk, Eric. No point in going over the past. What do we do now?'

'Let's see what the scan throws up. Be interesting to see her lie when her brain is lit up.'

Liddell switches on the closed circuit TV. He can see that Costello is already lying on the panel the nurse is manoeuvring into the scanner. When she is in he presses the mic button,

'Ms Costello, are you comfortable?'

A muffled 'yes' comes back.

'All right, just relax. We simply need to ask you some questions. Firstly tell us of your earliest memories.'

Costello relates an incident when she was four and was taken to see some fireworks. She was scared and her mother had to carry her home. She remembers that her younger brother was not scared at all and that she was intensely embarrassed and also upset to miss the fun.

'That's fine. Now tell us about what happened during the accident.'

'I told you I don't recall.'

'Just try very hard for us for the next couple of minutes, reach into that time. Do your absolute utmost to recall the incident.'

Richelieu magnifies a certain section of the screen,

'Well there it is, the Hocht pattern, clear as day. She definitely has some amnesiac trauma, maybe she's genuine after all?'

Liddell shakes his head,

'I still don't believe her; they just sent in someone with memory damage. They knew we would be able to tell.' He pushes the mic button, 'Hang on, Ms Costello. Now in as much detail, what are your first memories when you were in hospital after the incident?'

'My buddy Joel was there. He was reading a book. He didn't notice I was awake; I stared at him for a while. Then he smiled at me.'

Liddell taps the screen,

'Look at that activity over here, that's not a straight recall,' he flicks back to the first childhood memories and then to the most recent scan. 'She is thinking too much about what she is saying. It's not totally made up but some of it is guarded.'

'Yes, you are right,' Richelieu admits pressing the mic button,

'Ms Costello, please relax for a minute.'

Then letting it go he turns back to Liddell,

'So what do we do?'

'We have three options as I see it. Tell her we can't do anything for her and send her back; two, pretend to treat her or, three, actually give her the treatment.'

'What are your thoughts on the best option?'

'If we send her back it might provoke a bigger reaction. They might close us down, send in someone else, start some kind of investigation, who knows what? On the other hand if we keep her here it buys us more time.'

'I agree, let's admit her. And do we treat her?'

'Yes, let's treat her. To start with, it will make her a nicer person. It will also look less suspicious.'

The two doctors go into the scan room. Costello is sitting up sipping a glass of water,

'So how does the inside of my head look?'

'Almost as nice as the outside,' Liddell answers with a smile.

Richelieu gives him a look; the two sit down and Liddell opens her file,

'We think we can help. The treatment will take around three weeks during which time you will stay here.'

'I think I can manage that, especially if that Anton is going to be around.'

'You will need to take three pills a day. It is an as yet unlicensed drug so officially this is a clinical trial.' Liddell puts some official forms in front of her, 'You need to sign these documents of agreement to participation. We will also need to do regular blood tests and so on.'

'Are these drugs dangerous?'

'In the short term no. As for the longer term we think not, but have not had time to find out for certain; we do know the effects wear off within days if you stop the medication.'

'Fine.' Costello signs the forms.

Liddell hands her a notebook with lined pages,

'The first thing we would like you to do is to start filling in this memory book. We would like you to put down all your personal memories in here.'

Costello flips through the empty book,

'What, all of them, all my memories in this one little book? It would take ten of these.'

'I think you will be surprised just how few personal memories you have. Most of our patients get between one and two thousand.'

'Are you saying that I only have a thousand memories?'

'Yes, in terms of specific events. We don't include anything from the last six months or anything general, say, the seven times table.'

'It doesn't seem much for a lifetime – or should I say half a lifetime.'

'Let's say a third of a lifetime. Why not be optimistic? Actually you won't get many more and will lose more than you gain even if you avoid the dreaded dementia or Alzheimer's.'

'I still can't believe I have only one thousand memories.'

'You see, most of your life is made up of repetitive things. What do you normally have for breakfast at home?'

'Toast, honey and coffee.'

'Let's say you had that for the last year perhaps three hundred times – do you remember any specific breakfast among those?'

'Yeh, when the toaster went on fire.'

'So, that's one, any more, say breakfast number two hundred?'

'Well, not really, those breakfasts all seem to mush in together.'

'That's good, people without the ability to forget mundane useless details are usually in some mental trouble.'

Costello fingers the little book,

'So how do I go about it?'

'Most people start chronologically just working their way through their lives. Some go for a more themed approach say food memories, then places, then people.'

'OK, so I fill this in, then what happens next?'

'Well this provides us with a sort of template of where

you are pre treatment. We would like you to use the even pages only to start with. Once you start the course you carry on filling in on the opposite pages. We also want you to put down any memories you may get that you don't think are yours.'

'You mean like false memories?'

'Yes, the treatment can provoke certain kind of hallucinatory memories. With all this information we can tailor the treatment to the balancing point between bringing back the memories hidden by your trauma and minimising the memories that are not yours.'

'I'll get started right away. What about intimate stuff, do I put that in too?'

'It's up to you really. We are doctors of course; nothing can shock us.'

Liddell hands her a key and some documents,

'Your room, medication and test schedule. Make yourself at home.'

Costello goes to get her bag from her car. She sits in the passenger seat and gets out her cell phone.

Joel answers but does not say his name just a curt,

'Yes?'

'Good to speak to you too,' Costello says with a bit of an edge, 'I'm into the programme.'

'Excellent, any problems?'

'Everything's fine, they're a pretty nice pair actually.'

'Number one priority is to get me a sample of the drug.'

'But they're doing clinical trials, made me sign something, won't it be registered at the FDA whatever it is?'

'Something is registered but not what they are giving you

all. We tested it; it's a dummy.'

'Well,' Costello flicks through her schedule, 'I think they start me on it tomorrow. I'll do my *Cuckoo's Nest* impersonation. In the meantime I will check out the place. Security looks pretty lax.'

'Let me know what you find out, talk later.'

Costello takes her bag and finds her room. It is as luxurious as the rest of the building. After freshening up she gets the memory book out and heads for the terrace. It is still deserted, so she goes back to the spot she was in before and opens the book.

She decides to start with food memories. What was the first thing she remembers eating? Some little new potatoes with butter? How old, five maybe? Then some stringy meat at the school canteen, seven, an omelette with button mushrooms, twelve, and a glass of white wine, first avocado... She is scribbling away and doesn't notice a young woman maybe in her twenties coming onto the balcony with a cup of coffee cradled in both hands.

'Hi,' she says and Costello jumps again.

'Hey, that's the second time today. Does everybody here like to creep up on people and scare the bejesus out of them?'

'Sorry, didn't mean to startle you – you doing the memory book? I loved filling that in, it's just like when you going to die and all your life flashes up in front of you; plus, of course, you don't have to die.'

'Always a bonus, that not dying thing.'

'Yep, I find dying can really spoil things. I'm Mary Anne,' she stretches out a hand.

'Costello.'

'Nice to meet you, Costello.' She says the name with a slight wry smile but doesn't pursue any of the usual lines of inquiry and instead pulls herself backwards onto the wall surrounding the terrace. Costello flinches at her reckless behaviour.

The girl hoists one leg over and then the other so she is sitting with her legs dangling over the void below.

'Well, you're not scared of heights,' Costello says enviously.

'Not me, watch.' The girl puts her cup on the wall and jumps up and walks along the top of the narrow wall, even feigning a small wobble for added effect and jumping neatly over the sections of iron railings.

'How can you do that?' Costello marvels.

'It's nothing special, just regular walking along. People don't just fall over you know, well not adults. It's a design feature.'

'But if you did, just imagine.'

'I dunno, say you are walking along a sidewalk next to a busy road. You fall over into that road under a truck or a bus and you are just as dead as if you went down there. But you're not screaming and clutching onto streetlights as you walk along, are you?'

'I get what you mean but could you just sit down; you're making me nervous.'

The girl sits down; this time with her legs either side of the wall.

'You been here long?' Costello asks her.

'Two weeks.'

'Is it working, the memory stuff?'

'You bet. Not letting them know just how well. Don't want to leave this place, it's dreamy.'

'I know what you mean.'

'And you haven't had dinner yet. Just you wait. Maybe I could get some job here when I'm cured, cleaning or something?'

'How did you happen to lose your memory?'

'My uncle helped, he was a bad man. A bad, bad man.'

'Abuse?'

'Yep and some.' The girl picks up her cup, cradling it again.

'Wow, I don't know if I'd want those bad memories back.'

'You bet, I want to know every last detail. And let everyone else know, including him.'

'You getting some counselling?'

'Yep, a half hour a day with Lydia.'

'Lydia?'

'Doctor Liddell to you.'

'You call him Lydia?'

'Not to his face. Lydia and Richy Rich. They're sweet actually, in fact Lydia is quite hot.'

'I noticed.'

'But if the chips were down I'd go for Anton.'

'I hear there's a line.'

'You know about that already? You work pretty fast. You must be fifth in line, I'm number two I think.'

'Yep, I think Anton is the one to go for. When the kissing stops the cooking stays.'

'You made that up?'

'No, I read it in a book, *Red Dragon*.'

'Never heard of it.'

'It's good, but not his best of course. I'll lend it to you.'

'Thanks. Well, I'll let you get on with your homework.'

She jumps of the wall and skips off.

Twenty minutes later Costello has finished her food list, rounded off with a salmon she caught and cooked herself. She is not sure it was more than six months ago but she puts it in anyway. She counts them up, seventy-two, not a bad start. It has had the effect of making her hungry, plus there are definite signs of cooking aromas in the air. She looks round; the terrace is starting to fill up. She must have been engrossed. A couple of people give her a friendly smile or a wave.

Suddenly there is an expectant hush and she turns to see Anton standing in the kitchen doorway.

'Ladies and gentlemen, the soup of the day is lentil and the main course is braised lamb with the vegetarian option of Camembert parcels.'

'I want both,' someone shouts out.

'I want you, Anton,' someone else shouts, maybe Maybel.

Everybody laughs.

Anton continues ignoring the banter,

'Then a blackcurrant sorbet or cheese plate.'

There is a spontaneous round of applause and Anton does a little bow.

Mary Anne squeezes into the empty seat across from Costello and asks,

'Hello again – are you religious?'

'Nope.'

'You will be in a half hour. You will be worshipping our God of Food.'

Costello glances around at the various people.

Mary Anne leans over and whispers,

'Want me to tell you who everybody is?'

'Sure.'

'That lady,' she points to the first woman Costello met, 'is called Maybel but you have to be pretty careful.'

'Why is that?'

'These guys play tricks on you; say you ask is anybody coming for a walk, then they say maybe, you say well make up your mind, they say, we have, you say who is coming then and they say maybe. Very annoying, they mean Maybel but they call her by her nickname, *Maybe*. You got it?'

'I think so; I'll be careful.'

'That's Sylvie, talking to her, be careful too; don't turn your back.'

'Why?'

'Not saying, just watch out. Then those two are Delphi and Clare,' she points out two black women, one late thirties and the other, younger and model glamorous, sitting together on the other side of the terrace.

'Delphi is my top favourite.'

Delphi notices the attention and blows Mary Anne a kiss. Mary Anne stands up,

'I'm crap at this,' she tells Costello before kissing her hand and wildly blowing it towards Delphi. Delphi and Clare track the kiss across the patio before it is caught by the wind and blown off course. The two watch open mouthed as it does a couple of loop the loops and then as it swoops down past the ladies Delphi reaches out with a napkin and makes a spectacular catch. She opens the napkin, picks out the bedraggled kiss, pops it in her mouth and gobbles it down. Then she pats her tummy and gives Mary Anne a thumbs up.

Mary Anne sits down,

'She's funny.' She looks around, 'That's Joe, his dad owns

this place, he's fantastically rich. And right in the far corner is Markus, he don't speak much. I think he's a professor or something.' Mary Anne counts on her fingers. 'Somebody missing, oh yeh Lippi, he's always late. You'll know him, he's really tall. I always say to him 'What's the weather like up there?' when I see him.'

Costello's watch buzzes at three thirty a.m.

She pulls herself out off her deep sleep and curses momentarily.

(ALTMAN 32: you were never there if nobody saw you but people see with more than their eyes.)

She has a quick shower with perfume free soap. The shower has the added benefit of waking her up.

She puts on her dressing gown over her tee shirt and boxers and picks up her decoy mug – she will be searching for sleep-inducing tea if caught.

She puts her ear to the door, nothing, and then silently opens it. The corridor is dark but with just a faint glimmer of quarter moon filtering in through the large windows. She lets her eyes adjust and then sets down the corridor. Four minutes later she is outside Richelieu's office ready to pick the door open. She turns the handle – not even locked. She enters and closes the door.

She sits down at his desk and switches on his computer which asks for a password. Let's see, he was mostly middle of the keyboard. She heard six clicks. Head movement right left right and finishing left. Costello curses herself for not working on this earlier.

(ALTMAN 1: preparation 99 per cent plus execution 1 per cent equals success 100 per cent.)

I sure am rusty she thinks to herself.

Well it's going to be something French.

What about a French composer maybe? Debussy too long, Ravel too short, Satie too short, she tries ESatie. Nope. Painters? He likes art? Renoir worth a try, nope, she flicks through a mental list, authors, food, tries another seven – lucky there is no attempt limit on his software, French icons, what about Eiffel? Non. OK, do some research and come back later. She is about to power down the computer when she smiles ruefully, you stupid fool, this is to herself who is the fool, not Richelieu. She types in France and the computer springs to life. She quickly plugs a little hyper drive into the USB port and presses the clone button. It whirs softly for less than a minute sucking out the entire contents of the computer. She presses the 'erase access information' and the drive sets up a cookie that will delete any traces of what she has just done and then she shuts the computer down. A quick look through the desk drawers, nothing but stationery. So, let's see what Liddell has to offer.

His office is also unlocked. No computer here, just a monitor and connections for his laptop, which he takes with him everywhere. It's probably under his pillow as we speak.

Two grey filing cabinets immediately draw her attention. She approaches them and then stops herself short.

(ALTMAN 32: don't look before you leap – look before you look.)

She takes a tiny flashlight out of her pocket and meticulously examines the cabinets. Ah, two small hairs perched on the top lip of both top drawers. One could be an accident – two probably not. She momentarily worries about the door she has just come through but consoles herself that it would be impractical to have examined that in the corridor.

She removes both the hairs after making a mental note of their exact locations and places them carefully on a table. With these old cabinets she won't even need her picks. She puts her hands on either side of the first one and squeezes it gently. Come on she tells it. The cabinet clicks satisfyingly and she pulls the top drawer open.

It is full of folders each marked with a patient's name. She flicks through first of all for her folder. Unfortunately but unsurprisingly not there. Could be one of the doctors still has it. Would have been good to check what they were saying about her. She pulls open the next drawer and pulls out Joe Klein's. She unfolds the scan-wand and quickly drags it over each of the pages in his folder. She chooses the files of a couple of other patients at random and quickly scans them.

The third drawer is empty. Not big believers in paper these two. Oh well. Save the planet.

She shuts all the drawers and carefully replaces the hairs where they were before. Then slips out of the office. She feels vaguely that she has betrayed the two doctors' trust. Perhaps the fact that they didn't even bother to lock their doors has tweaked her conscience.

She heads back up the dark corridor to her room and is momentarily congratulating herself on the perfect mission when she hears a woman's echoey voice from the pool room,

'Hey, come on in, the water's lovely.'

She looks into the dark room. In the moon gloom she makes out the head of Sylvie who Mary Anne had warned her about that morning. With her hair licked back and in the moonlight she looks almost seal like; isn't there some legend about a woman turning into a seal? Or the other way round?

'Couldn't sleep, was just looking for some tea.' Costello holds out her mug as proof.

'I got a lot better than tea. Over there on that chair, sweetie.'

Sylvie points to a small jug with a single cocktail glass next to it.

Costello goes over and sniffs the contents.

'Margaritas?'

'You bet, help yourself.'

Costello tentatively pours some into her mug.

'You want some?'

'Can't let you drink alone.'

Costello fills the glass and takes it over to her. She is still in the water with her elbows on the side of the pool. Costello hands her the glass and dangles her feet into the pool. It is surprisingly warm.

'You can't sleep either?'

'Nope, just love to swim, especially when the pool is empty. Who would've believed that before I came here I hadn't swum a stroke? Totally scared of water. Now, watch this.'

She puts her glass on the edge and disappears under. No bubbles or anything. Costello puts her mug down worried.

Suddenly Sylvie surfaces at the far side of the pool.

'Impressive huh?' she calls over and then does a leisurely crawl back to Costello's side.

'Seriously, you couldn't swim before you came here?' Costello asks.

'Nope, not a stroke. Know what Little Joe thinks?'

'Joe Klein?'

'Yeh, we call him Little Joe. Klein means little in German, but he also reminds me of one of the guys in *Bonanza*. He was called Little Joe, the nice one.'

'Don't think I've seen it. What does he think then, our Little Joe?'

'He thinks they're turning us into X-men with their pills. You know giving us each special skills as well as the memory back.'

Costello tries to visualise Richelieu and Liddell as Xavier and Magneto – unsuccessfully as it happens even although she has a vague recollection that Magneto was called Eric by Xavier at some point in one of the films.

'So your special skill is swimming; what's Joe's?'

'I won't spoil it for him; you'll find out soon enough. Why don't you come on in, race you across and back?'

Costello slips off her dressing gown and slips into the water. She is a pretty fast swimmer, highschool champion, very fit and this novice with a couple of margaritas in her should be no match.

'Let's make it two double lengths freestyle?' Costello says.

'On your marks, get set, go!'

Sylvie sets off and Costello pushes off immediately but simply can't catch her.

Two lengths later Sylvie is back at the start point as Costello puffs up.

'Now for my prize,' Sylvie says shaking the water from her hair.

'We didn't mention prizes, what is it?'

'A kiss, of course.'

'I don't do that sort of thing; I'm strictly boys only, sorry.'

'Me too before I came here.'

'Whatever those doctors are giving you, it's certainly life changing all right.'

'I know, I know, but it feels good, feels positive.' Sylvie floats on her back. 'You sure about the kiss?'

'Yeh I'm sure.'

'I'll ask you again in two weeks; bet you'll have changed your mind.'

Costello pulls herself out of the pool; she is conscious of Sylvie staring at her breasts showing through the wet t-shirt,

'You do that, see you tomorrow.'

'See you.'

Costello sits in her car and calls Joel.

'How long you been there now?' he asks her.

'Four days.'

'We got the pills you sent and the professor's computer clone.'

'Any use?'

'Nothing interesting on the computer; I think all the good stuff might be on Liddell's. Any chance getting that to us?'

'I can try; he always keeps it with him, like a mother and baby. Plus he has a thirteen step password with non-standard characters. I need to get at it when it is up and running. What about the drug?'

'Well it definitely is a prion. But it's not what they registered. Something about the folding of the molecule is different. We can see what it looks like but can't replicate it; that's why we need to get Liddell's data. What about the other patients, you got any more out of them?'

'It's all pretty confusing. They are definitely memory-improved if that is the right word or even a word. But something else is going on. New skills, mood changes, personality differences. I think the only way for me to find out for real is to start taking the medicine myself.'

'It's a risky strategy; what if it affects your personality? What if they start manipulating you?'

'Well in that case you can write me off and send in someone else. As if you hadn't thought of that already. On the other hand I might be able to tell you what is going on, first hand, from the horse's mouth.'

There is a long pause. Costello is just about to think the connection is broken when Joel answers.

'All right, start taking it, but if you feel you are losing control I want you out of there fast.'

'OK.'

There is a sudden knock on the car window. It is Maybel,

'Say, Costello, Richelieu is looking for you. He's in his office, looked a bit annoyed.'

'Better go,' Costello tells Joel. 'The principal wants me.'

'You remember what I said, watch out for yourself.'

Costello wonders if Joel really does care about her – he has that habit of switching on you.

Costello goes into Richelieu's office. Liddell is sitting on his boss's desk.

Richelieu doesn't look up from his notes but simply says,

'Ms Costello, apparently you have not been taking your medicine.'

(ALTMAN 99: when faced with the truth be truthful.)

'No.'

'Why not?'

She wonders whether to sit down or not; they haven't asked. Standing makes her feel even more like a bad pupil,

'I was scared. I wanted to hear more from the other patients before I started. Looks like some of them are having some pretty weird reactions.'

'You mean the personality changes and hallucinations?'

'Yep.'

'Well you have to understand that most if not all these people, including yourself, have been through extreme experiences. When we lower their protective defences mood swings are inevitable. The hallucinations we gradually bring under control. You should have talked to us about your worries.'

'I'm happy to start taking the medicine now.'

'You are absolutely sure?'

'Yeh. Positive.'

'As we said before, if you feel unhappy with the changes, we can stop treatment and they will simply wear off.'

Liddell opens his laptop and keys in his password. Costello counts carefully without looking; yep thirteen strokes and many of them holding down at least two and sometimes three keys. That is definitely not France.

He enters some information then shuts the laptop and jumps down from the desk.

'Let's go and see nurse Hendrix.'

In the dispensary Liddell informs the nurse of Costello's misdemeanour.

'Apparently naughty Ms Costello has not been taking her medicine.'

Costello is starting to feel like a five year old.

Hendrix shakes her head and tuts.

'But I gave them to you here?'

Costello opens her mouth and shows the bottom of her tongue.

Hendrix laughs,

'Oh that old Jack Nicholson has a lot to answer for, doesn't he?'

Then to Liddell,

'You want me hold her nose and massage her throat while you give her the pill?'

'I thought you could shoot them down with a peashooter.'

Costello holds up her hands,

'OK, OK, I promise to eat your goddam pills.'

Liddell tells Hendrix,

'We need to reset the tests and start the programme from scratch.'

'No problem, you still got the original pills, honey?'

'Sorry I flushed them away.'

'Not to worry. Well, here we go again.'

She tips out one of the little white pills into a plastic container and Costello swallows it, afterwards voluntarily opening her mouth for examination, even lifting her tongue,

'All gone.'

Next morning Costello gets to the deserted terrace five minutes before Liddell normally arrives.

(ALTMAN 28: when following someone always stay in front.)

She arranges herself on a sun lounger and closes her eyes.

He arrives on time as usual and sets up his laptop and puts his funny wrap-around dark glasses on.

Costello looks over,

'How can you possibly see your screen with those on?'

'They're special polarised glasses I made myself – they actually help me to see the screen in bright sunlight.'

'How's that work?'

'Come over and I'll show you.'

Costello gets up and walks to the table.

'Look, light from a computer screen is polarised in one direction, it's all lined up in parallel if you like. These glasses have polarised lenses which let light through in only one direction. If I turn them 90 degrees like this the screen goes black.'

He twists the glasses and the screen behind them does indeed become completely opaque.

'But when lined up properly they let all the computer screen light through, one hundred per cent.'

He twists them back ninety degrees and the screen is clear.

'So you cut out half of the glare from the sunlight but none of the computer screen light? Pretty smart, you should patent them.'

'Too late, I already told you, my secret's out, premature disclosure. I'd imagine somebody else has already thought of it anyway.'

Costello has been hoping to see something useful on the screen but it is an Internet bird-watching site. Still that gives her a useful in to the plan she has been hatching.

She moves across to the wall and looks over,

'I saw the cutest little yellow bird ten minutes ago hopping around. Had a sort of greyish-black cap.'

Liddell looks vaguely interested,

'Hmm, could be quite a few species.'

She has hooked his interest, now to start winding him in,

'Had the sweetest little black bib and olive coloured wings, about this size.'

She describes the dimensions of the bird with her hands.

Liddell is standing up now,

'Where was it you saw it?'

'It hopped into that bush way down there. I think it had a friend, maybe a girlfriend?'

Liddell goes over to the wall and, shading his eyes from the sun, starts peering down at the bushes below.

Costello places herself between him and his computer and behind her back slips the hyper drive into the USB slot and presses the 'clone start' button. The drive starts humming softly but Liddell is oblivious to the sound.

'What was its beak like?'

'It had a straight little pointy one. Made a kind of insecty tweeting noise.' Don't get too particular or detailed, she reminds herself.

'You seen it before?' she asks him.

Liddell is now leaning dangerously over the wall,

'Nobody's seen it for years if I'm right. It must be a Bachman.'

'Bach what?'

'Bachman Warbler. Shouldn't be this far north. Too dry up here for them.'

Costello keeps her hand on the humming drive, the whole scene has a sort of pantomimeish quality to it; she feels like shouting he's behind you.

Liddell crouches down and looks through the railings,

'More south California or maybe Carolina. They've been extinct for thirty years as far as anyone knows. I better get my camera.'

He rises and turns sharply and Costello has just time to pull the drive out of the computer slot, hoping its copying was complete.

Liddell snaps his laptop shut and picks it up,

'Have you got a camera on your phone?' he shouts from the doorway.

'Yep.'

'If you see it again take a picture, take lots of pictures. I'm going down there.'

He hurries off and Costello feels a double wave of guilt – exploiting his childish passion for something feels totally wrong. Also she feels a pang for the poor little warbler, briefly resurrected, but in actual fact dead as a dodo. She silently imagines the last one flitting around some dried up swamp looking for a friend and finding none before expiring under some bush. She clutches the small drive, mission successful but it gives her no pleasure.

Several times during the afternoon Costello sees Liddell down in the scrub to the side of the valley with his camera and binoculars, looking like some long lost explorer, Dr Livingstone I presume. Once he notices her and gives a wave before making a hapless arm gesture. She feels especially guilty when she transmits the clone of his drive to Joel.

That evening after dinner he appears at her cleared table with a whole set of large glossy cards each with a picture of a different bird printed on it. He spreads them out before her.

'Which one of these did you see this morning?'

'It wos him wot done it guvnor,' she says pointing to the Bachman Warbler card. 'I'd recognise his ugly mug anywheres.'

Liddell scoops up his cards quickly.

She notices his embarrassment and says,

'I'm sorry, didn't mean nothing.'

Liddell taps the cards to align them into a neat bundle.

'I must look a bit of a dope with this obsession.'

'No, not at all. In fact it is quite attractive. I like passionate men. Why don't you let me take you out for a drink to make it up to you?'

Liddell thinks for a moment,

'Where to?'

'Paradise Cove maybe, do you know it? Probably some interesting terns down there, maybe an albatross?'

Liddell laughs,

'OK, but no more talk of birds. I sometimes take this bunch down to that place. What about drinking and driving?'

'We just drive down the canyon drive to the freeway, park this side and play chicken across the road. On the way back there will be nobody to run into and the worst we can do is drive over into the ravine.'

'That does sound like a plan.'

In the Mustang Liddell carefully belts up.

Costello watches him in amazement,

'We're not taking off you know?'

'You'd be arrested in England driving like that,' he answers flapping her unused seatbelt.

'Scaredy Cat,' she tells him.

Costello has parked on a small rise and lets go the brakes without starting the engine. The car eases down the slight slope and she turns into the narrow road. On the steeper slope the car gradually picks up speed. Somehow without the engine the silent drive feels scarier and the car more out of control, like a runaway train. Speed builds up pretty fast and Costello seems to relish each of the many hairpins hardly touching the brakes. Liddell braces his legs against the dashboard.

'Scared of driving?' Costello asks.

'Scared of dying, more like.'

At the bottom Costello does a spectacular circular halt throwing up a cloud of dust.

'Let's get you that drink, you sure look like you need it.'

The Paradise Cove is not too busy and the two get a table with a sea view. Liddell gets a double whisky and Costello a Martini,

'I been trying to think who your name reminds me of and it's just come to me.'

'Go on,' says Liddell warily.

'*Chariots of Fire*, the Scottish runner.'

'Otherwise know as the flying Scotsman.'

'Da da-da-da dah dah.'

Liddell joins in,

'Dah dah do-do daaaah.'

'So are you named after him?'

'I was named after the original runner, not the film. I was born before that came out.'

'Thought you were English not Scottish?'

Costello notices that Liddell's foot is touching hers under the table, though maybe just accidentally. She thinks about moving hers away but decides to leave it for the time being.

'The Americans and the French for that matter don't usually make a distinction there. I'm actually half Scottish. My father was from up there and I spent most of my childhood in Scotland too.'

'You don't have much of an accent, I mean a Scottish accent. I saw that *Train Spotting* movie; they had to have subtitles for it over here.'

'Shudi go'a hale bo'l stedi this wee glass. Mno rite?' Liddell says in his best Glaswegian.

Costello nods impressed,

'I got just the one word glass and that's it.'

'What I said was I should have got a whole bottle instead of this small glass, am I not correct?' This time he invokes a strangled Prince Charles accent.

'What happened to the word bottle?'

'Basically in Glasgow the ts are replaced with glottal stops, a kind of grunting. It's the strange combination of lazily dropping the consonants reducing everything like I said to grunts coupled with the puzzling activity of the tongue to produce the rhotic rs that gives a kind of snarl to the words. Grunts and snarls. I'd like to think if you heard cavemen talk they would have sounded rather Glaswegian.'

'Well I can't imagine the old cavemen or should we say cave people talking like your queen. Imagine them saying – pass me my stone axe would you there's a dear, I'm just going to chop this old dinosaur's head off don't you know?'

'The dinosaurs died out 60 million years before the cavemen – I mean cave people – came along,' Liddell corrects her.

However, Costello has the perfect answer ready and can

hardly wait to say it,

'She could've been about to cut off the head of a fellow caveperson whose views were rather old fashioned hence the appropriate use of the word dinosaur.'

Liddell admits defeat,

'There's no arguing with that. I stand corrected, the use of the word dinosaur in that context was exemplary.'

Liddell's foot is still touching hers, with maybe an experimental extra pressure. She decides to return it.

Liddell goes on the verbal offensive,

'Anyway you can talk about incomprehensible accents. Look at the way you speak over here.'

'It's perfectly normal, natural and a delight to the ear.'

'What about when you say boo-ee.'

'What the hell's wrong with that, how do you English say it?' Costello uses the word English in a rather pointed fashion which Liddell ignores.

'We say boy of course.'

'But its spelled b-u-o-y. Isn't it French or something? We are merely trying to preserve our multicultural inheritance.'

'But you don't say he was boo-eed up.'

'I think we should start that tradition, in fact I would be rather boo-eed up to have another Martini, don't you know?'

Liddell comes back with a couple more drinks,

'What did your parents do?'

Costello screws up her face,

'They were martial arts instructors.'

'What, both of them?'

'My mum retired pretty soon after she had me. Dad nearly got into the National squad; he was State karate champion for three years.'

'And you?'

'Never liked it really, used to referee when they fought though.'

'Your parents?'

'Yeh, it was just for fun, nothing personnel, till one day she accidentally gave him a black eye. I'll never forget the sound of that blow, ouch. He never heard the end of it from the club; they called him panda boy after that, always making cracks about who wore the pants and telling him he'd better get home and make the dinner or she'd do the other eye.'

Costello gives an extra squeeze on the foot that has mysteriously returned to the same spot it was before and they both laugh.

'What a pair we are, playing footsie like a couple of teenagers,' Costello says.

'And aren't you meant to do that with lots of people around who don't realise what's going on? We have nobody to hide from here,' Liddell replies.

'Maybe ourselves,' Costello concludes.

Half way up the drive back up the canyon road Costello pulls into a passing point overlooking the valley below. You can still faintly hear the sea. She leans over and kisses Liddell. It lasts a good few minutes. She surfaces at last,

'Handy these seat-belt thingies, meant you couldn't get away so easily.'

'You felt me struggling then?' Liddell replies.

He undoes the belt and this time leans over for the difficult second kiss – will it manage to surpass the first, without that element of surprise and novelty and expectations that the one before raised? Nevertheless, both seem happy.

'Let's lie on that flat rock?' Liddell points a large smooth stone.

Costello agrees,

'Good idea, I need to top up my moon-tan.'

'You need to be careful with getting a moon-tan,' Liddell cautions. 'If the moon is not fullish you get a little pale crescent down the side of your face.'

'That would indeed be foolish.'

They lie down on the stone which must have been absorbing heat all day and is now radiating it back through their clothes and balancing the cool night air above.

Liddell looks up,

'You can always come back to get the complementary bit of tan to the old sickle moon when its waxing or waning, which is which, I should know; maybe I have had too much whisky?'

'No idea which is waxing and which waning. It's like ebb and flow, difficult to distinguish.'

'Like up and down or in and out.'

'Exactly.'

Costello kisses him and then rolls on top,

'Are you going to get in trouble for this, you know the patient doctor thingy?'

'Strictly speaking you are under the care of Dr R. I am only assisting him. It would be frowned upon definitely, not exactly best practice. What about you?'

For a moment Costello wonders if he knows who she really is and who she is working for, and is almost tempted to tell him. Then she remembers her day's work; tricky to explain to someone you are kissing that ten hours ago you secretly sucked the contents of their computer from them while sending them on a wild goose chase, or rather warbler chase. Go with the flow for now and a good moment to tell him will crop up she thinks unconvincingly to herself.

In the meantime you need to answer she recalls,

'Why should I worry? I never heard of a patient being struck off.'

Just then the moon disappears behind some clouds and at the same time the breeze stiffens from the sea. Costello shivers,

'Damn, there goes my tan.' She rolls off the top of Liddell and pulls her jacket round herself,

'We should be getting back to the ranch.'

The rock too is beginning to lose its heat.

Liddell nods,

'I think I'll walk from here, it's not far.'

'Good idea.' They stand up. 'One for the road?'

'*Say nighty night and kiss me.*'

After their last kiss Costello jumps in the car. She winds the window down and leans out,

'*Sweet dreams till sunbeams find you*,' Costello sings to him, she has a sweet voice.

'See you tomorrow.'

'Arrivederci amore.'

After she drives off Liddell doesn't start walking but goes back and sits on the cooling rock hugging his knees and looking down into the valley. The moon comes back to keep him company; there is a very thin veil of cloud, which it shines through easily so that it looks as if it is on this side and much closer. Liddell almost feels he could pluck it out of the sky like an apple.

'*Dream a little dream of me*,' he finishes the song.

Costello wakes with a start. Too much information. She tries to sort out reality, from dreams, from hallucinations. Well the business with Liddell last night could have been a dream but wasn't. Part sneaker her can't believe that she could be so dumb as to get involved like that but at the same time she has a kind of warm feeling when she thinks about him. Then the rig explosion, well that was true all right. It feels as if a spotlight is playing around the incident lighting up odd corners here and there. She remembers Fairs being shot now, that wasn't in any report, he died in the explosion officially. She remembers the shock of the cold water when she jumped off the rig or was pushed rather. And then the dream, was it a dream? A space like California, but not California, not at all, open, light, bright but different too and different sounds. Also a name, a new name she has never heard before but has known all her life, her own name?

On the terrace over coffee she struggles with updating the memory book. She needs to give the doctors an update on the accident or they will think she has stopped the medicine again but she can't tell them what she is actually remembering. She has to fabricate some equivalent that matches her cover story. Let's give them the place stuff in the hallucinations section she thinks. Unlike a fading dream the place memories seem to be strengthening by the minute.

Liddell sits down suddenly at the table.

He makes a wry face.

'Good morning,' Costello says, she almost feels in shock to see him in reality again. 'Or maybe not such a good morning?'

'Probably not such a good morning. I'm off to see the boss.'

'You going to tell him about last night?'

'Yes, tis a far, far better thing I do. I don't want to compound the sins of commission with the sins of omission.'

'Will he be mad?'

'Well he certainly isn't going to give me a cigar and a big bear hug, that's for sure.'

Costello blows him a tiny kiss,

'Good luck and hey don't forget,' she sings,

'*You must remember this, a kiss is just a kiss.*'

Liddell joins in,

'*A sigh is just a sigh.*'

He gets up to go,

'Was it just a kiss?'

'That's for me to know and you to find out.'

Costello watches him leave and the warm feeling is back.

Liddell goes into Richelieu's office, who has three case files in front of him on his desk.

'Something of a delicate situation has arisen,' Liddell hesitantly starts.

Richelieu looks up at him slowly,

'I like your use of the passive tense here.' Richelieu opens his hands like a flower blooming and adopts a slightly sarcastic tone, 'It simply arose by itself, this situation, with no encouragement from either you or Costello?'

Liddell sits down,

'You know what I'm talking about then?'

'Just an observant guess really. It was hard to tell which of the two of you was most desperate.'

'Now, now.'

'So let's just clarify a few details. You are starting some kind of affair with one of your patients who we also suspect might be a secret agent spying on you or rather us. Sounds like extreme unprofessionalism on both sides to me. It will end in tears, I guarantee it.'

'Maybe it wasn't me who fell for her?'

'You or Alfredo, it doesn't really matter, you have to take collective responsibility for both your actions. And that raises a whole set of issues we haven't really dealt with. It appears we have a certain homosexual interest arising among our patients.'

'I'm not sure it can be called homosexual, in a way it is heterosexual as well.'

'Shall we just say that the barriers are blurring.'

'And existing relationships are challenged.'

'And you seem to be conducting your own personal experiments now.'

'These things do happen, what can I say?'

'You can say, I will end this here, there is too much at stake to let some flirtation jeopardise it.'

Liddell bites his bottom lip.

'Eric?'

'OK, OK.'

Costello sits down next to Joe Klein.

'You're Joe?'

'And you're Costello – I heard about you.'

'I heard you had a special X-men skill.'

'Who said that?'

'Sylvie.'

Joe tears a page out from the back of his memory book and rips it into a neat square.

'What's your favourite animal?' he asks Costello.

'I don't know, a kangaroo, say?'

'All right,' he starts folding. Two minutes later he holds up a perfect paper kangaroo. Costello peers at it closely,

'Look, it's even got a little baby in its pouch.'

Joe gives it to her.

'I'm just guessing you couldn't've done that before you came here?' Costello says turning the little animal around.

'Nope.'

'Not sure just how useful that special skill is going to be in the X-men wars though?'

'That's not really my number one special skill,' Joe tells her.

'What is then?'

Joe shows her his memory book.

On one page are written his memories in English rather scrappily while on the opposite page is what looks like Japanese calligraphy, immaculate and very beautiful.

'You speak Japanese as well?'

Joe gives her a quick burst of Japanese.

'What the hell did you say?'

'Just a short poem about how beautiful you are.'

Joe leans in closer to Costello and whispers,

'You know this stuff the doctors are telling us about hallucinations?'

'Yep.'

'I'm not sure they are, you know, hallucinations.'

'What do you think they are then?' Costello realises she is whispering too.

'I have a strange feeling I was somebody else once, this Japanese guy.'

'What d'you mean, like a sort of past life?'

'Yeh and the medicine lets me remember it.'

'You tell them, the doctors?'

'Course, but they just said it was common what I felt, like my brain trying to make sense of unrelated memories. They reduced my dosage to half and it's fading a little, the Japanese memories. That's why I'm trying to get everything I can remember down. You got a computer here. Can you check some stuff out for me? I can't work these things too well, I tried but…'

'Sure, I'll see if I can, give me the details.'

Joe writes down a Japanese name, a street, a town, some dates.

'See if you can find if this guy existed and whether he was a teacher.'

Costello folds the paper.

'I started to have similar feelings myself, a name, a place, nothing I can put my finger on yet.'

'Wait, there's something else, two kids who I can't get out of my mind, and a woman.'

'They got names too?'

'Yeh, my imaginary friends, sure, let me write them down; they are all Japanese too.' He adds the three names to Costello's sheet.

Costello tries to do a search on Joe's information on the web but can't get anywhere, so she emails it all to Joel.

A day later she phones him from her car.

'You get the stuff about Joe's hallucinations?' she asks.

'Yep, except they're not hallucinations. That guy Taniguchi lived all right, died around a year before Joe was born. We had the same sort of thing with Liddell trying to find out some info on a Mexican guy. Looking at the dates I guess he was checking out some past life he had himself.'

'You mean to say this Japanese guy is now our Joe, like a sort of reincarnation thing?'

'Sounds a bit weird but that would explain not just the memories but the whole speaking Japanese and paper folding. Are you getting anything like that yet yourself?'

'Something but nothing checkable so far, just vague feelings.'

'Better keep taking the tablets then.'

'If this is really working in the way you think then it's massive. It changes everything.'

'More than you can possibly imagine,' Joel sounds distracted.

'What about them other three names I gave you from Joe?'

'This Japanese guy had two kids, one still lives in the same village, something like a postmaster, the other's at Tokyo University, high flyer, literature.'

'And the woman?'

'She was his wife. Killed herself at his graveside seven months after he died.'

'Pretty sad. Shall I tell him all this, Joe, I mean?'

'Better not, we had to send somebody in Japan to the town itself to find out this information; it's not anything you could've got on the Internet. If you tell him it might just raise suspicions with the doctors. Just say you couldn't find out anything on your computer – it's true enough.'

Costello goes looking for Liddell. She sticks her head into the games room and peers around. Clare and Delphi are playing pool.

'Nobody in here but us coloured folks!' Delphi shouts out.

Costello goes in to the room,

'Are you allowed to say that?'

'We is, you ain't. Come on in and give us a game. I'm fed up whooping Clare's ass.'

'Why don't you play her at pool then?'

Clare and Delphi both laugh.

'You don't mind playing with poor white trash then?' Costello asks.

'No, come on over you white trash.'

'Hey, you're not allowed to say that, only me.'

'Touché,' squeals Clare poking Delphi.

Delphi ignores her and hands Costello a cue,

'Come on Cosy, show us what you got.'

Costello takes aim and satisfyingly knocks several balls in. She silently thanks her misspent youth.

'Lucky,' comments Delphi.

As Costello is lining up her next shot Claire asks her,

'How are your memories going?'

'I was talking to Joe; he didn't seem sure about this old hallucinations business.'

Costello finally misses and Delphi takes over playing fast and accurately; another misspent youth Costello imagines.

'Joe, he's a little dope, sweet but not that bright. Believes everything those doctors tell him,' Delphi answers between shots.

'What do you two think about the whole business then?'

Clare answers for them,

'Well for a start those ain't hallucinations; they're real lives. Why I can remember places, smells, lovers…'

'The smell of lovers,' Delphi joins in putting her nose high into the air. They all laugh.

'What about you, getting anything yet?'

Costello answers,

'I only been on it a couple of days but this has come to me, listen.'

She sings a little ditty in some foreign language which sounds like it comes from Africa with those tongue-clicking sounds in it.

Delphi puts down her cue in astonishment,

'Saints above, that ain't even African American, that's African African. You one of us, girl.' Delphi puts her arms round Costello in a bear hug.

'You understand that language?' Costello asks the two of them.

'Course not, but I recognise it, it's from down south of Africa like Swahili or what's that one that starts with an X.'

'Xhosa?' suggests Clare.

'Yeh, that's the one, Xhosa. You know, Costello, what we been thinking about all this, you know when everybody gets it the prion things – this is the end of racism.'

Costello picks up her cue again,

'Haven't we done that with all that business already, I mean aren't there laws and equal rights and everything?'

'Sure we can sit on the bus next to you and go to college; we even had a goddam black president, didn't we?'

'Wish he was still here instead of the asshole we got now,' interrupts Clare.

'Amen to that. Yeah but getting back to my point – you still can't say when I walk into a room that you don't react to the colour of my skin. Now though when all this gets out, half the white people will have been somebody non-white and half the black people will have been white. You won't know who you are talking to. Why for all you know that Prince William himself could have been just recently running around naked in the jungle with only a couple of leaves tied to his Willy Wonka.'

'I think he maybe did that anyway in this lifetime. You know those weird schools those rich Brits go to,' Clare clarifies.

'That's true enough,' Delphi admits.

'So who were you two, you know... before?' Costello asks.

Delphi does her breakfast television voice,

'Cosy, in my previous life I was Haaken, Norwegian fisherman.'

'And, Cosy, I was Jo Hallestrom, a black African American, just like now but she was rich,' adds in Clare.

'Yeh?'

'Yeh, still trying to remember where she hid her jewels; I mean our jewels.'

'So you can speak Norwegian?' Costello turns back to Delphi.

'Yeh and she can speak posh,' Delphi answers pointing at Clare.

Costello is back at the table now,

'So you half him then, this Haaken guy?'

'No I'm still old me but with lots of his memories and sometimes he almost seeps into me, you know opinions and stuff. I'm thinking differently. Sneaks up on you, if you know what I mean?'

'Yeh, the whole thing has a sort of x-files feel to it,' Claire adds. 'I even saw some Star Trek thingy where they put this little worm in people and it had all kinds of memories of past lives that came with it. Confused the heck out of everybody. They didn't know if they was talking to the new person or the old one, girl or boy, old or young; there was a lot of past lives in there.'

'Yeh but at the same time it feels kind of normal, like something you've always known, just at the back of your mind,' concludes Delphi, anxiously watching Costello coasting through the final balls.

'That's five dollars you owe me,' Costello tells Delphi after picking off the last ball.

Delphi reluctantly puts a bill on the table,

'Double or nothing? Say, you got the hots for Lydia?'

'What is this place? You don't get any privacy around here?'

'He was looking for you half an hour ago.'

'Maybe I should go.'

'Let him wait. Absence makes the heart grow fonder. Besides, I need to get my money back.'

Costello enters Richelieu's office with a certain sense of déjà vu. Richelieu is behind his desk; Liddell is sitting on the windowsill – this time with his feet up on the edge and his arms round his knees – he has an aversion to chairs Costello thinks. Liddell ignores her and studiously looks out the window.

Costello sits down without waiting to be asked. This time she will be treated like an adult.

Richelieu clears his throat and then,

'Ms Costello, is that your real name?'

Costello nods.

'We don't think you are who you say you are.'

'No?'

'We think, in fact, we know that you are some kind of agent.'

Costello looks over at Liddell but he keeps looking out the window.

(ALTMAN 190: when faced with your outing, play along, there is much to be found out in your own outing.)

'Yep, you could say that,' she answers calmly.

'CIA, FBI?'

'I was in the FBI but after that was recruited to a special force managed by Joel Krista about three years ago.'

'Krista? I have never heard of him.'

Liddell speaks for the first time,

'He's something to do with the President, a shadowy character, helped with the President's election campaign. There was an article in Time Magazine; what was it? The Forgotten Man. Never got a big place in the government despite many people thinking he managed single handedly to get the President elected.'

Costello leans forward,

'Shadowy is right, but not forgotten, in fact he is the government. You ever seen that video of a basketball team where they ask you to count how many times they bounce the ball? Then afterwards you say fifteen or so, maybe sixteen bounces and then they ask you: what about the guy in the gorilla suit? And you say, what guy? And they run the video again and sure enough this guy in a gorilla suit runs right thrtough the middle of the players grinning and waving at you and you say, how the hell did I not see that guy? That guy in the gorilla suit is Joel.'

'How does he do it?' Liddell asks.

'It's like a magician thing. It's to do with distraction; a conjuror takes your attention elsewhere so you don't see what the hands are getting up to. Joel is the hands. But now we are putting all our cards on the table, maybe you can tell me what you two are really doing?'

Liddell looks at Richelieu who nods in a resigned sort of way and Liddell carries on,

'Well, as you probably realised what we have termed 'hallucinations' are as far as we know real memories of past lives. The hallucination idea was not meant to cover that up, just to let the patients develop the memories without thinking that was what they were supposed to be doing. We didn't want to put the idea in their heads.'

'We wanted to see if they just came up with it themselves.' Richelieu clarifies.

'So everybody who takes your pills comes up with a prior life memory?' Costello asks.

'Everyone so far, which is only nine including yourself and Liddell. We think that there is potential for not just a single memory but many. If we increase the dose we go further back into more and more lives. We have only tried that with Liddell here and it started getting confusing so we pulled back on those higher doses for now.'

'So what are your plans, you two, you want to give this to everyone in the world?'

'First we need to find out more, safety is a big issue. We don't want to wipe out the whole population or drive them mad. We want to do a large controlled test. Does this Joel you work for have access to the President? Maybe he could help us organise it.'

Costello tries to grasp what is happening. Her whole allegiances are shifting, with her past memories, the business with Liddell, perhaps mostly the whole enormity of the situation. This is not some little scam in LA; this is a world-changing event. She realises that the doctors are waiting for a reply,

'The first thing to do would be to convince them that this is for real – at the moment I guess they think it's most likely an elaborate set up, maybe using hypnosis or some kind of auto suggestion, coupled with drugs etc.'

'Why would we do that?' Liddell asks.

'Same as anyone else, to make money, you know how big the astrology business is. You get some high profile publicity, set up a company, by the time people realise it doesn't work you are sitting on a small or maybe even a big fortune.'

'Do you think this is a scam?'

'No, I'm trying to give you a picture of how they are most likely seeing it. Of course I don't think it's a scam, but remember I'm starting to live it. Listen, if I went to Washington I'm pretty sure I could convince them that it is real, get you your tests. The whole set up.'

Liddell looks questioningly at Richelieu who shrugs in a kind of 'it's out of our control' way before telling Costello,

'OK. We thought we would have to work our way up through a mountain of bureaucracy to get to that point. But it might be good to start at the top. We have certain conditions for the tests of course and also we have some safeguards in case things don't work out.'

'You better fill me in then.'

After the meeting Costello walks aimlessly round to the large garages at the back of the estate. A tall skinny white guy is playing basketball with a hoop on one of the garage doors.

He throws a long shot which drops straight through without touching the sides.

Costello applauds and he turns. The ball rolls up to her and she tosses it back to him,

'Hey, I'm guessing you couldn't do that two weeks ago?'

'Hey yourself, I sure could. I've been playing professional the last two years. You don't watch much sport on TV do you?'

'No, I get out too much. Never knew we had a star here, what's your name?' Costello asks although she remembers it from her conversation with Mary Anne,

'Fernando Lippi. Want my autograph?'

Lippi bounces the ball a few times and then without even saying catch, he throws it to her.

She catches it and nearly falls over from the force.

'Careful there,' she says slightly winded.

'Sorry I didn't know you didn't know how to catch a ball,' he laughs.

'I caught the friggin ball all right,' Costello holds it up as proof.

'You didn't catch it, you killed it stone dead, that ball is now dead meat.'

Costello looks at the ball,

'What d'you mean, dead meat?'

'You sucked all the life out of it, I give it to you with momentum and spin and now it's got nothing. Throw it back.'

Costello throws the ball with as much force as she can, trying to wind him back. He simply palms the ball behind him and swings it round again to the front where it is now spinning on his fingertip.

'The energy for the spin, you put that in, not me. Let your opponent do all the work.'

Or your enemy Costello thinks to herself,

(ALTMAN 230: consider tripping someone, compare the tiny energy you put in and the damage caused, let your adversary supply the energy.)

'What's that about damage caused?' Lippi asks still spinning the ball.

Costello checks herself for thinking out loud, must watch that in future.

Lippi bounces the ball a few times,

'Hell, I don't want to cause any damage, just get the ball in the basket.'

'I know, it's just I think you hit on a universal principal that applies to everything from wars to kissing.'

Lippi throws another perfect shot.

'Don't you ever miss?' she asks him clapping softly.

'Only when twenty thousand people are watching.'

Lippi pretends to throw the ball to her again but stops himself.

Costello winces.

Lippi does one more throw and then asks her,

'Say, why don't we get a coffee, you can tell me more about that kissing business you were talking about?'

Costello follows him thinking, this time definitely to herself,

'Oh, oh, here we go again.'

Joel ushers Costello into the Oval Office,

'Mr President, this here is Special Agent Costello.'

Joel never knows in these circumstances whether he should complete the other side of the introduction. After all everybody knows the President. But when he doesn't finish it, it hangs in the air. Must be a protocol book somewhere around, probably with ten pages about visiting ambassadors, kings, emperors, other presidents.

They all sit down on three sofas, one each.

'Joel has briefed me on the whole situation at KARC and what they seem to be doing. Seems you have uncovered quite a scheme.'

'Not really uncovered; they weren't hiding it.'

'To be honest, we're not convinced. This could just be some elaborate hoax or worse a con. Plenty of mileage and money to be made out of persuading people they have past lives, I guess.'

'Seven hundred and twenty million dollars in the last year alone, just in the USA,' Joel adds.

'Sir, I assure you this is absolutely for real,' Costello protests.

'I'm afraid we are going to need something a little more convincing than just your say-so, honey.'

Costello looks the President in the eye and gives him a burst of Xhosa replete with clicks.

'Well that is certainly impressive but what the hell is it?'

'It's Xhosa, a language from South Africa. I didn't speak it till two days ago.'

'Well it's Greek to me,' the President jokes. Joel laughs politely but Costello fixes the President with her steeliest Clarice Starling look and he gets up and goes to the door,

'Sarah, angel, we need a translator, immediately, some South African language?'

He turns back to Costello,

'How do you spell what you just said?'

'X - H -O - S - A.'

'You got that?' he asks the secretary. He comes back into the room,

'Might take some time. So how is young Joe Klein Junior doing these days?'

'Well, he speaks Japanese now.'

'Hell, you got yourself a little old language school up there.'

'The language thing is only a fraction of what is happening. It's a whole lifetime of experience you get.'

'Have those two been doing any form of hypnosis on the patients or some type of suggestion? False memory stuff?'

'No. A couple of the patients with abuse-based-memory-loss have been getting counselling but the rest of us just get three pills a day and regular medical checks. We are pretty much left on our own.'

'Any news on that translator?' the President calls through to his secretary.

'We found a Rev Q... Q...' she stumbles.

'Just spell it for us.'

'Q -o -b -o -z -a?'

'Qoboza,' says Costello.

'Yeh, that's it, he teaches at a nearby school, car already on its way sir,' she shouts back.

The President turns back to Costello,

'So while we are all waiting here, what about the Carlson Affair, any idea of what actually happened down there? Have they managed to retrieve your memories?'

Costello looks back and forth between the two men; she has deliberately said nothing to Joel about what she has recalled; she wants to see his face and the President's when she tells them,

'Apparently they were expecting us, Fairs, my second in command, got shot just after we boarded the rig, two others immediately injured. I decided to abort the mission and when I called in for back up to get us off – it appears that the bombs we were carrying were remotely armed.'

Joel looks Costello directly in the eyes,

'The munitions had that capability, but it was only ever meant to be used in case of a total wipe out of the task force; it should never have happened while you were still active.'

Costello thinks to herself that she should have known that Joel would be unphased by the question. Slippery, slippery.

The President, however, is looking quizzically at Joel,

'We armed the bombs? Didn't they go off accidentally?'

'Whether an accident on site or whether someone here accidentally misunderstood the protocol is more or less irrelevant. What is important is that a key strategic goal was achieved, and we should be thankful to those men and women who gave their lives for it.'

Most were my buddies, thinks Costello to herself. Two months ago she would have been shouting it at the two of them, but she is calmer these days. She has a wider perspective.

The President's secretary eventually ushers in a very dishevelled and surprised looking teacher.

'Reverend Qoboza' she attempts, the Reverend nodding in a 'well that's probably as good as one would have expected' kind of way.

He turns to the President and Costello realises that he

is in a state of shock. Well she herself was phased when she came in and she had time to prepare and knew why she was here.

'I am not sure what I am doing here, is there a problem?'

Joel moves in like oil on water,

'No problem, Reverend, we are very grateful for your coming at such short notice; all we want you to do is converse with this young lady in Xhosa. Take a seat please.'

The Rev Qoboza looks at her in surprise as he sits, but before he can say anything Costello sits down on the sofa next to him and launches into a tirade of Xhosa.

The Reverend answers, laughing and patting the back of his head.

'What did she say, Reverend?' asks the President.

'She said I looked like I had been dragged through a bush backwards, but in slightly more colourful terms.'

'Carry on.'

Costello and the Reverend talk for a good ten minutes. At one point they even sing a little song together. The clicks in the language reverberate round the oval room in an eerie way.

Eventually the President has had enough,

'Ms Costello, could you wait in the study?'

Costello nods and stands up with a flurry of farewells to the Reverend.

After she has gone Joel asks him,

'Well it is pretty clear she speaks your language; how long would it take her to learn that?'

'A lifetime, how old is she? Thirty? She must have lived her whole life in South Africa, idioms, turn of phrase. She could never have learned it in this country.'

'Definitely more than, let's say six months?'

The Reverend doesn't hesitate,

'Definitely.'

'You have been a great help to us. A car will take you back to where you were before and we will of course pay you our daily translation fee.'

The Reverend Qoboza nods graciously. As he is going out he says,

'One strange thing which does not make any sense to me in view of her age; she speaks in a rather old fashioned way, a few of the newer words she stumbled on, it felt as if I were talking to my grandfather.'

'Did you happen to ask her how she knew how to speak the language?'

'Of course, I thought maybe she had been brought up in one of the villages. She refused to say though. Funny, if I closed my eyes I would swear she was black.'

After he is gone the President says to Joel,

'Curioser and curioser. I'm still not convinced by this smoke. Maybe she has been learning this stuff for a long time.'

'She got this job less than a month ago.'

The President sits down, he looks a little tired,

'Untangle this goddam web for me Joel.'

'Well it's looking like two possibilities, either these guys have stumbled upon something that really does unlock past lives and we happen to have seen a pretty convincing demonstration here, or else they are up to some extraordinarily elaborate ruse. If it's the latter, I can't believe Costello would be in on it, so they have somehow convinced her. And why would they do it? They are sitting on a pot of gold with the Klein family; he has thrown money at them.

What would they have to gain? If this is a fabrication, their reputations will be in tatters when it comes out.'

'Hokum, Joel, I still smell hokum. You said that Costello had some proposal from them.'

'So she said, but also that she would only tell you directly.'

'Get her back in,' the President sighs.

Costello comes back in still grinning,

'Hey, I can't tell you how much fun that was. Did I pass the audition?'

The President is not amused,

'According to the good Reverend you do have a detailed knowledge of that language but as far as how or why, well Ms Costello, let's just say that we are still not convinced. Not convinced but not unconvinced. Joel said you had some kind of proposal to discuss that you wouldn't share with him alone?'

The three go back to their sofas. One each again.

Costello takes a deep breath,

'OK, this is the deal, what Richelieu and Liddell would like is a publicly funded open trial of the prions in LA with ramped participation eventually leading to a trial with five thousand volunteers, including stringent safety checks. Then if all goes well...'

The President stops her,

'Hold on young lady. I think these are decisions we should be making. This is starting to feel a little like the tail wagging the dog.'

Costello gets a little flustered here and blurts out,

'If they don't get the go-ahead for the trial on their conditions, the alternative is they release the information on the web worldwide so anyone can make the prions.' As soon as she has said it she realises it was a mistake. The President has already stood up and is confronting Joel,

'The alternative? Is this a threat? Are these people threatening us?' There is a strain of incredulity in the President's voice.

Costello tries to backtrack,

'No, no, not at all, it's not a threat; we really want to work with you and your government…'

The President seizes on the stray pronoun,

'We? Are you hinting that you are now part of their team? I thought you were working for us, Agent?'

A couple of weeks ago being shouted at by the President would have turned Costello into jelly. But somehow she, or rather they (for she is a they now) are remarkably calm. She holds his gaze.

Joel steps in and whispers in the reddening President's ear. The President nods and gives a sign for Joel to take over before moving over to stare out of the window.

Joel comes and sits next to Costello,

'Listen. Let's go one step at a time; let's get the facts straight. We are all on the same side here. Firstly, have your doctors already posted this information, how to make the prions, what they think they do, etcetera, on the web? I'm presuming it is presently inaccessible?'

'Sure, at present it is hidden; it needs a daily input to remain that way so if anything were to happen to anyone it would become available immediately.'

Joel smiles in a relaxed way,

'Happen to anyone? Come on, Costello, this is America you know. Things don't just happen to people here.'

Costello does not reply to this, but Joel carries on anyway

as if she had assented,

'Now, releasing this information like that can't be a good thing; I'm sure that is not what your doctors would like. Think of the chaos that would result. We still don't even know if it is safe.'

'No, we agree that is a last resort.'

'So you all want this public trial, and you are? How do you fit into all this now?'

'Like a go-between, liaising the project. This is going to change the whole world.'

'I think we get the picture. I need you to go back into that nice waiting room while the President and I talk it through.'

He takes her by the arm and whispers to her as they walk to the door,

'This could have been much easier if you had let me know all this in advance.' It is the closest she has ever seen Joel to losing control.

He closes the door behind her and approaches the simmering President who bursts out,

'I can't believe it; this is blackmail! Why don't we just send in the marines and lock them all up? Get hold of their computers, shut them down. We have computer people, we run the Internet for God's sake.'

'I understand how you feel, sir. But we have to act prudently here. If what she says is true it is possible that we couldn't stop the global release of this information. And the consequences of that…'

'So what do you suggest, simply give in to their demands? It's blackmail, plain and simple.'

'What we want is control of the situation. This whole thing could be useful to us, fine; if not then we want to extinguish it cleanly and quietly. Let's suggest a compromise large test on our terms, military personnel in a closed camp. Then we can verify it, find out the consequences and plus it will buy us time to try and see how to stop the web release of the information.'

The President has had enough,

'OK, OK Joel, you're usually right; you sort out the details. I don't want to see her again, ever.'

Costello pulls up the drive of the Institute. It has been a long day and she is not relishing telling the news she is bringing. She wonders which of the phrases don't shoot the messenger or between a rock and a hard place best sums up her situation. Maybe this is how a ping-pong ball feels. It is just growing dark. Liddell is sitting on the steps waiting for her. They observe the no contact rule. He raises his eyes in a questioning way.

'Good news and bad news,' Costello tells him.

Liddell gets up with a sigh,

'Thought it might be. We better find the boss.'

Costello follows him into the building and through to Richelieu's office. Richelieu is sitting at his computer. He puts his finger to his mouth and indicates the gardens. They walk round the pond in the twilight.

'Could be some little listening devices back in there even you don't know about,' Richelieu explains.

'Wouldn't surprise me,' Costello admits. 'But you believe it's safe out here? Ever take a look inside one of those roses?'

'You're serious, aren't you?' Liddell asks.

'Yep, but don't worry; we have nothing to hide. They know what I am going to tell you anyway.'

'So what did your beloved President say about our scheme?' Richelieu asks.

Costello ignores the pointed 'your' and answers,

'You're not going to like this. Firstly I think I convinced them about the prions and everything. They even found me someone to speak Xhosa with.'

'What was that like?' Liddell asks.

'You know what, it felt like going home,' Costello smiles.

'So they believe it works.'

'Well possibly. Enough to sanction some more experiments. Big ones.'

'You said there was some bad news.'

'The bad news is they won't let you do it here in LA, or in public. They want to do it on their own terms; they want to be in control. National security and all, they imagine what you are doing could have strategic importance, military outcomes, you know.'

'That makes sense. What are the details?'

'Firstly, they want to move the whole centre to a closed military camp in New Mexico. Total news blackout from now on, not a peep about what this is about. The subjects of the initial experiment are to be a thousand soldiers.'

'What about the current patients?'

'They come too. Everybody. Containment, they call it.'

Richelieu, who has been silent all this time, finally joins in,

'Well, we need to discuss this.'

'I don't think we're talking options here,' Costello tells him.

'We could refuse to co-operate.'

'Well, who knows where that would lead. They could certainly close this place down; you must be breaking dozens of federal laws here. How are your tax returns for a start? And that's just using legal methods. You two and me as well, could disappear in the blink of an eye.'

'What was the good news again?' Liddell asks.

'Well listen, why not go along with the proposal? Sure you lose some home comforts, but working with the soldiers, what difference does that make? Could be interesting – you already have a ton of background material on them; think of it as a control group.'

'I just don't like them being in control.'

'Well if you agree to co-operate reluctantly you will have some bargaining powers. They have agreed to let me be involved as go-between.'

'And whose side are you really on?' Richelieu is getting steadily redder. Costello can't get the similarity of his reaction to the President's out of her mind. She imagines the two of them red faced in a field banging their horns together.

'Hang on,' warns Liddell. Costello realises Liddell is the equivalent of Joel in this parallel universe – talk about Through the Looking Glass.

Costello speaks some Xhosa. Something about the sound of the language and the authority it is delivered with calms everyone,

'What does that mean?'

'It means family is everything. Remember, the pair of you, whoever I was when I first came here, I am not now. That goes for those thousand soldiers. After two or three weeks they will be – well they will be a thousand international citizens of every type. It's brainwashing in the most positive sense; they end up with better, cleaner brains with much more in them rather than less.'

Richelieu is definitely calmer but has one last go,

'What's to stop us just releasing the information on the web and be done with it?'

'You two can do that at any time if things start going wrong. This way you get to add more information, you get to control the experiments and if you do put it out into the ether, God knows what kind of chaos could happen, what kind of misuse. You still don't even know if it's safe.'

Liddell puts his hand on Richelieu's shoulder.

'She is making sense. This way we stay in control.'

'I don't trust them.'

Costello senses a breakthrough,

'No, we shouldn't. But this is pretty scary for them too.'

'I need to talk with Liddell, alone.'

Costello turns and heads back to the Institute,

'Fair enough. I'm getting used to being put in the quiet room.'

After she has gone Richelieu shakes his head,

'Can we trust her? You should have gone to Washington.'

'We needed her to convince them. Plus she's changed. She is not the person who turned up here two weeks ago. You should take the prions yourself. You have no idea how it alters everything. You become a richer person.'

'Someone has to stay out of the loop. What if some side effects suddenly turn up? I think we should stall them. We need a public announcement of the trials to protect ourselves.'

'We have the Internet sites. If they try anything and I don't log on, everything goes public. They won't risk that.'

'Let's sleep on it. Tell Costello we will decide in the morning.'

At three in the morning Costello is woken by hammering on the door. She opens it and sees a fire-fighter going down the corridor banging all the other doors. He is shouting,

'Everybody out.'

Costello asks him what is going on.

'Wildfire. It'll be he here in less than five. Road's already closed.'

Out in the courtyard two fire helicopters are standing their blades still spinning slowly.

Clare and Maybel come rushing out in their dressing gowns.

Costello sees Richelieu and Liddell surveying the blaze from the terrace.

Liddell turns to her,

'Accidental?'

'Unlikely, in view of the timing.'

'Are they trying to close us down?'

'No, it's more of a warning shot, a small encouragement to accept their generous offer.'

'It looks like we don't have much choice.'

Richelieu turns,

'We could simply walk out. Go back to Europe. Start up again over there.'

'What about our patients – we just walk out on them?'

'They will be fine. The memories will fade; they will be no worse off than when they arrived here.'

Costello shakes her head,

'You two believe you could get out of the country?'

‘What would they do?’

‘Legally as I said they could probably find twenty reasons to arrest you. And then in the realms of the illegal the possibilities are endless.’

‘You mean put us somewhere like Guantanamo used to be?’

‘No. Guantanamo was visible. That’s the tip of the iceberg sticking out of the sea; you have no idea of the real stuff. Play their game – it gives us time, plus we gain a thousand allies. It’s a lot harder to disappear a thousand than three.’

Suddenly they are bundled into the helicopter and quickly rise above the Institute which is in a neat little circle of calmness surrounded by raging fires. A too neat circle, Costello thinks, waving a silent goodbye to her car as they head down towards LA.

NEW MEXICO

Costello and Liddell stand outside the door of the mess hall with Lieutenant Greenway; it is late afternoon and they are about to meet their first bunch of test candidates.

The speed of the transfer to New Mexico has taken Costello's breath away. Only the patients, herself, the nurse and the two doctors have transferred. Anton has been sent back to France, much to Richelieu's annoyance.

The Lieutenant pushes open the door, glances into the room and does a quick headcount,

'They are all in there, your first batch; you sure you won't want me to come in with you? They can be just a little frisky.'

'I think we can manage,' Liddell reassures him.

The Lieutenant gives them each a sheet with passport size

photos of the soldiers with their names underneath,

'Any real trouble just note their names down.'

Costello and Liddell enter the mess hall; around twenty-five soldiers, about two thirds male, are sitting at the tables.

Costello starts with a cough to quieten them,

'Ladies and gentlemen, I am agent Costello and…'

'Where's agent Abbott?' this comes from a soldier at the back.

Costello under strict instructions from Greenway to take no nonsense asks him,

'Soldier, what's your name?'

'I'm soldier now; a minute ago I was a gentleman.'

'Name?' Costello takes out an official looking pad and licks the end of her pencil.

'Private Lewis, aww please don't tell the lieutenant; I didn't mean no harm.'

He has put his hands together in prayer and has everyone laughing with him.

'Well just this once Lewis. As I said I am Agent Costello and this handsome man here is Doctor Liddell.'

Costello sits on the edge of the table,

'Now what your President would like is for some of you to volunteer to take some experimental drugs.'

Some fake smacking of lips noises go round the room,

'Like LSD or ecstasy?' says what looks like Private Lewis's best friend.

'Much more fun that those two old chestnuts; these will really blow your minds.'

'What are they then?' this is from a tall guy with glasses. Do soldiers wear glasses? Costello wonders momentarily.

'They happen to be some special prions that Doctor

Liddell here has developed.'

Tall with glasses carries on; he must be the brain box of the troop,

'Those the things that make cows go mad?'

Crew-cut in the middle with tattoos, adds,

'Yeh, will we all end up talking nonsense and falling over?'

A big guy to his side pushes him onto the ground shouting,

'How would we tell if they had any effect on you?'

'I guess this is what he meant by frisky,' Costello whispers to Liddell, 'maybe you better explain the differences between your prions and the BSE ones.'

Liddell nods, takes up a piece of chalk and approaches the blackboard,

'So, we all have the endogenous PrP proteins in our…'

'Hey, doc, why don't you cut the big words; give it to us like five year olds.'

Liddell thinks for a minute, then,

'OK, we all have some proteins in our heads that are folded to look like this say,' he draws a wiggly line. 'Along come the big bad mad cow proteins that look like this,' he draws a saw edge line. 'They get close to the good ones, really close, and turn them into the bad ones which turn others into bad ones. Then the bad ones clump together and destroy your brain. With me so far?'

The soldiers generally nod and Liddell continues,

'My prion is folded like this,' he draws an extra wavy line, 'and tends to make the proteins it comes into contact like itself too, just like the bad ones.'

'So how do we know your nice little prion whatsit won't destroy our brains too?' tall guy/glasses.

'Two things, first my prions don't like to clump together

and more importantly they are not protease resistant like the…'

'Hey, you're doing it again, big words man,' arises a chorus from the soldiers.

'Sorry, five year olds, I forgot. You all have in you helpful cleaners that munch up proteins, the baaaad mad cow ones they can't eat so they fill up your brain, whereas my nice ones they can. So if we stop giving you mine, why after less than a week no trace of them can be found; they've all been munched up.'

Liddell has been illustrating on the blackboard as he speaks and it now looks like some crazy Pacman massacre has taken place.

A question from Lewis at the back,

'Wait, will we grow boobies?'

One of the women soldiers at the front says,

'If so bring it on,' holding her arms out.

The soldier to her right tells her.

'What you complaining about? You got plenty there.'

Only to be met with a terse,

'I ain't heard anyone asking for less.'

'And that's just the women,' big guy joins in.

Costello takes control again,

'All right, simmer down now. Are there any real questions so far?'

'So what do these drugs do?' tall guy with glasses again.

'To be brief, they bring back memories of your previous life.'

There is a little silence.

Then,

'Like reincarnation, they reincarnate you?' this is from

boobie welcomer.

'A bit like that, but to be exact what we have discovered is you are all already reincarnations; you just can't remember. The drugs let you remember who you were before.'

A serious looking guy who looks too young to be in the army, Costello guesses twelve maybe thirteen, asks,

'What if we were something else like a monkey, say, you know in our previous life, that would be a bit weird?'

Costello nods to hand over to Liddell who answers with,

'So far in all those we have tried it on everyone's past life has been another person.'

Costello can't help herself but butt in with,

'But to be fair on the other hand we have only tried it on humans so far,' and gets a pretty big laugh.

'So is it like some relation you come back from – I had an uncle everybody says I look like,' Lewis shouts.

'Poor guy,' from crew-cut/tattoo.

Liddell gets up,

'No, so far the previous lives have borne no relationship to the person experiencing them. In fact they seem random so it is unlikely that more than one of you will have a previous incarnation from the USA. From this group as a whole we expect the likeliest outcome would be three Chinese people, one USA as I said, one west European, two Indian, three south American and five African.'

'It's the United Nations.'

'Well in a way this will show us how united we really are.'

Lewis yet again,

'I have a feeling I was an Italian count before.'

'I didn't know there was an o in that word,' Costello can't place the speaker; general laughter.

'What about male or female?' This is from a woman soldier with her hair in two little bunches.

Liddell carries on,

'Once again, the gender of your past incarnation appears to be random and not related to what you are now, so slightly higher odds you would have been female. In fact your likeliest bet is to have been a Chinese woman.'

'But what if you was somebody famous before like Elvis or Monroe or Einstein?' Crooked nose, Costello labels him instantly; she is getting the hang of this,

'Well then, soldier, you have hit the jackpot; you can sell your memoirs, but unfortunately that is extremely unlikely. There are simply not that many famous people around.'

Crooked nose does not agree,

'Sure, there are plenty around.'

'Where are you from?'

'Texas.'

'OK, a little experiment. All of you name some famous Texans. Come on, give me some names.'

'Red Adair, fireman oil well fires, from Houston.'

'Alvin Ailey,' from the baby boy.

'Who the fuck's he?' from Lewis unsurprisingly.

A chorus of tuts from the female soldiers greet the expletive.

'Pardon my French ladies,' he apologises.

'Hey, fuck isn't French,' Lewis best friend turns to him in combative mode,

'Sure it is. What about le fuck, or donnez moi un coup de fuck?'

Having made his point Lewis turns back to the original question,

'So who the hell is he then, this Ailey guy?'

'A choreographer.'

This is greeted with a chorus of oohs and bent hands,

'I can't help it if I'm cultured,' baby boy complains.

A chorus of names come from all corners of the room.

'Gene Autry.'

'Bonnie and Clyde.'

'Joan Crawford.'

'President Eisenhower.'

'That guy in Dallas?'

With each name Costello puts a chalk mark on the blackboard striking through each four to make groups of five.

'Ben Hogan the golfer.'

'Buddy Holly.'

This last elicits a short chorus of that'll be the day from some at the back.

'President Johnson.'

'Janis Joplin.'

'Tommy Lee Jones.'

The names are coming less quickly. Quite a few have given up but some stalwarts soldier on.

'Roy Orbison.'

'Dan Rather.'

One soldier who hasn't spoken till now stands up and salutes,

'Admiral Nimitz,' he starts singing '*Oh say can you see,*' but is quickly shushed and pulled back down.

'Robert Rauschenberg.'

'Rip Torn.'

Someone else asks is that his real name? No it was Elmore apparently.

Costello puts up her hands to stop them but it is not really necessary, their brains are emptied of the famous Texans. She looks at the list in a derisory fashion,

'Less than twenty and that is in a population of what, around twenty million say? So it's a thousand to one, even if we treat the whole camp, that we come up with a celebrity. Any other questions?'

'What if you were somebody real bad, like say Adolf Hitler?' Grace Jones look-alike.

'Well the chances you were Adolf is around six billion to one and also that presumes that he didn't die in nineteen forty-five but survived till twenty years ago.'

'Why's that?' tall glasses.

'So far everyone's previous incarnation has died within a year of their current birth. And I'm guessing none of you are sixty years old?'

'Feel like I am sometimes,' boobie welcomer.

'You certainly look it,' her friend from behind who immediately apologises.

'But what if you were some anonymous bad guy, a paedo or something?' Grace Jones again.

'My guess is that your current experiences would allow you to come to terms with your past, you become a bigger person. Listen it's not like another being popping up in your head; you will still be you, the same as the ten-year-old-you was still you. In the worst case, if you couldn't cope, we can simply stop the drugs and the memories fade away fast, almost like dreams.'

'I got a question,' tall/glasses again. 'Isn't it a fact that more people are being born than are dying, so there shouldn't be enough people from the past for everybody? I heard that only fifteen people ever lived for each of us now.'

This takes Costello by surprise but Liddell is on top of it.

'That's one of the things we would like to find out with this larger test. You are right, population is going up and was even more so twenty years ago. There is maybe a one in hundred chance that one of you won't have a past life.'

'Would you take it?' baby face.

'Both Agent Costello and I have already taken the course and I think we would both agree it has been life enhancing.'

Costello nods.

There is a long silence.

Costello finally breaks it,

'So now you all know the gruesome facts, who's in? The scheme is entirely voluntary and deciding not to participate will not affect your careers in any way. Maybe we could have a show of hands?'

A few hands go up at first. Then a surge,

'Why not ask who's not in, that'd be easier?' shouts out Lewis.

'All right, who's not in?' Costello asks.

Silence again, then all the hands go down.

'Hell lady, we're all in.'

Liddell produces a bundle of consent forms,

'Well, ladies and gentlemen, thank you for your time. We have some agreements for you to sign and we will start medical tests at the med centre tomorrow at ten.'

The soldiers line up to sign and Costello starts writing her own snapshot names on the sheet of photos.

'What are you doing?' Liddell asks.

'Learning their names.'

She hands him the sheet,

'Test me?'

Liddell folds it so the names are covered and points to one of the women soldiers,

'Private Greys.'

Liddell checks,

'Correct, how do you do that?'

'It's a magic trick thing; you just make up a story connecting the name and a feature. She was the boobie welcomer; I just imagine her with grey boobies.'

Liddell tries another,

'Him?'

'Private Brewer, he was the tall one with glasses; I have a little picture of him brewing some beer and whoops, drops his glasses in the vat.'

'You are weird. I wouldn't like to be inside your head, especially once we have done the whole thousand of them. By the way the famous Texans was a nice touch; we should keep that in for next time.'

'Yeh, broke the ice a little.'

Outside the mess hall Costello and Liddell meet five of the old inmates from the clinic. Joe and Lippi are missing but Costello is surprised to see the normally reticent Markus with the four girls. Delphi shouts out at Liddell and Costello,

'Look, it's the star crossed lovers.'

The five are all wearing military camouflage outfits. Mary Anne does a twirl for Costello, who asks her,

'Didn't they agree you could keep all your civilian stuff, you know, clothes and everything here?'

Mary Anne nods,

'Yeh, but hey, we want to join in the fun. Blend in, a soldier's life for me.'

'They wouldn't give me a gun,' moans Sylvie.

'Thank the sweet Lord for that,' Costello tells her.

'You know, I was thinking of getting my head shaved like that JI Jane,' Clare butts in.

Costello sighs and shakes her head sadly,

'Where are you all going anyway?'

'We have discovered the bar at the other end of the compound,' Mary Anne says excitedly.

'Cool.'

Maybel sings or rather chants – she is obviously the sergeant in charge.

'We are go-in to a bar.'

The rest join in as a disharmonious rabble.

'WE ARE GO-IN TO A BAR.'

'And we gon-na have a drink!'

'AND WE GO-NNA HAVE A DRINK!'

'You coming with us?' Maybe asks.

Costello shakes her head,

'You go ahead and we'll catch you up; we have some things to discuss.'

'You just don't want to be seen with us,' Delphi says.

'Is it that obvious?'

'You be good now,' Clare adds.

The little group take up formation and trot off in unison singing their ditty. There is quite a bit of bumping and laughing in the ranks.

'A happy little band,' Costello remarks.

'Yes, you wouldn't think they had half their possessions burnt up and then been allocated to virtually a prison camp.'

'I think this whole memory thing changes you. You get such a broad perspective on life. Your mortality is lifted off you. Why not be happy?'

Costello and Liddell slowly head through the camp for the bar.

Costello puts her arm through Liddell's,

'But if knowing your past makes you happy, a better human being, why does your body suppress it? Why do we need your drugs in the first place?'

Liddell thinks for a while,

'Richy and I have discussed this quite a lot and we have slightly differing viewpoints. In general we both think it might be something to do with evolution. Survival of the fittest. This transfer of knowledge gave an advantage up to a certain point in animals.'

'I thought you said back in there, in the mess hall, that this was a human thing, no monkeys blah blah.'

'What I meant was we think, and so far the empirical evidence supports this, that humans have past human lives. This is one point Richy and I diverge; he thinks this is a humans only thing, part of what makes us different. I am not convinced though. I think it must be species related though, so I'm pretty sure our chums won't inherit rat memories. But we have no knowledge if this happens in animals.'

'Might be a touch difficult to test.'

'Indeed we could give a pussy cat some of our prions, that is if they work the same way for them as humans, but how would we know if they worked? Say the poor thing remembers a life as some Australian cat, big deal, all we end up with is a confused cat. And that might be the answer to your original question. At that level the initial knowledge kick-starts the learning process, sets up certain learning routines etc. but beyond that specific memories are just confusing or even disadvantages to reproduction for example confusion about sexuality.'

'So the brain suppresses them after a certain age?'

Liddell nods.

'But what about our happy troopers from Santa Monica? Aren't they better off now?'

'Well maybe happier but evolution isn't really interested in happy, just passing on the old genes. I don't know if we have given that lot any survival advantages; indeed there appears to be a marked interest in homosexual activity for a start.'

Liddell and Costello enter the bar. Their little group is huddled together and seem to have made a good start on the alcohol. Maybel shouts out at the two,

'We seen Lid and Cos up a tree,

K - I - S - S - I - N - G.'

With all the group joining in on the I N G.

They pull up some extra seats and scrunch up so the two have no option but to join them.

Maybel starts the ball rolling,

'Say, Lydia, didn't RichyRich tell you to keep your sticky fingers off of PATIENT Cosy?'

Liddell looks accusingly at Costello, who shrugs,

'What can I say? Girl talk, they should be working for the CIA; they could prise information out of anybody.'

'Yeh who needs water boarding? Haven't they heard of six gin and tonics?' Maybel says turning back to Liddell,

'So?'

He answers cautiously,

'Ms Costello is not officially my patient; we are colleagues.'

'Yeh I heard that Cosy was more an IMPATIENT than a

patient,' joins in Delphi.

Costello spots a distraction to rescue Liddell,

'Hey, Maybe, that cute soldier is staring at you.'

Maybel looks over,

'He is cute.'

Costello recognises the private; it is baby face.

'His name is Private Calder,' she tells Maybel then adding to Liddell, 'Told you it would come in useful.'

Maybel gets up and approaches the private,

'Hola, weren't we at school together; what was your name again, Calder wasn't it?' The private looks slightly puzzled but not unwelcoming.

'Go get him tiger,' Delphi shouts across the room.

'Cradle snatcher,' Clare adds in for good measure.

They study the minicourtship unashamedly as if they were watching a baseball game.

Five minutes later Maybel comes back to the group to pick up her bag,

'Private Calder is going to show me his rifle.'

Clare pats her on her back,

'Well you give it a good polish girl.'

Delphi passes the bag up,

'What's his first name?'

'Don't want to know; I like it formal, you know,' she salutes smartly, 'Stand to attention – Private Calder.'

'Well you keep him away from your privates,' Delphi tells her.

'Fat chance of that,' Clare adds.

Maybel leaves arm in arm with the private winking back at her comrades.

On their departure attention swings back to Liddell and

Costello.

'What's it worth to keep Richy in the dark about you lovebirds?' says Sylvie rubbing her fingers together.

Costello tries for a second time to turn the attention away from her and Liddell by asking,

'None of you ever talk about your relationships; you're not all nuns are you?'

Delphi snorts and then answers,

'Well I got a no good husband, but he is simply not worth talking to, with or about. Maybe as we saw likes to play the field, no strings; Clare here is too old and ugly to get anybody.' She says this last with a touch of envious irony.

'Speak for yourself, Fatass,' Clare tells her before carrying on with the list,

'Old Lippi is happily married to some cheerleader and they got two beautiful children; probably writing her some long love letter right about now. Little Joe, well we all tried for him, cute, inheritance, but he is definitely distracted by something else.'

'Or someone else?' Delphi adds.

Costello remembers the information she got from Joel about the Japanese trio, maybe it's time she passed it on to little Joe.

'Richy, nobody has a clue, maybe he is not even human. Sylvie here has come over all queer since she started the memory stuff, haven't you?'

'Won't give us girls any peace at all,' Mary Anne adds.

'Kiss me! Kiss me!' screams Clare and the whole table collapses in a heap of laughter apart from Sylvie who says crossing her arms firmly,

'You know you want it, only a matter of time.'

When they have recovered Delphi puts a maternal arm around Mary Anne,

'And this sweet little thing is too young and innocent to even know what we are talking about.'

Mary Anne squirms under the arm,

'Hey, I done it. Loads of times.'

'Course you have, Honey, course you have,' soothes Delphi shaking her head sadly at the rest of the group.

Costello looks at Markus.

Sylvie explains,

'Him, we know nothing, he is an en-ig-ma.'

'I have nothing to say and I am saying it,' Markus obviously quotes.

'John Cage?' asks Liddell.

Markus nods.

'That the guy from Ally McBeal? I love that show.' asks Sylvie.

'Not him, no, the real John Cage, the composer,' Liddell clarifies.

Costello puts her fingers on either side of Liddell's head,

'One a these days this is going to pop with all of that stuff inside it.'

Liddell puts his hand on his heart and recites solemnly,

'The brain is wider than the sky,
For, put them side by side,
The one the other will include
With ease, and you beside.'

At the end he kisses Costello's hand and gets a small round of applause from those round the table.

'Who wrote that?' Delphi asks.

'Your greatest poet, Emily Dickinson.'

'I thought our greatest was Walt Whitman?' Sylvie says.

'Hell, I thought it was Bob Dylan,' Clare adds.

'No way. Emily is tops,' Liddell affirms.

'So who's your greatest poet then, Robert Burns?' Costello asks him.

'No Alexander Montgomerie.'

'Give us a line?'

'My hairt is heich aboif,
My body full of bliss
For I am sett in luve
As well as I wald wiss.'

'In English please,' Delphi pleads.

'My heart is high above,
My body full of bliss
For I am set in love
As well as I could wish.'

'Ah, sensitive, smart and with a job. If you don't want him, Cosy, step out of the way,' Delphi proclaims.

Eventually Liddell and Costello leave the bar to a chorus of be goods, be carefuls and enjoys.

It is dark, new moon and away from any city light pollution the sky is bright with stars, and a couple of planets.

Liddell points them out to Costello,

'Jupiter and over there Saturn.'

'You are a human Wikipedia. I guess you probably even know the names of the trees just by looking at their leaves?'

'Possibly,' Liddell admits.

'Show off, you think you know everything don't you? Wait a minute; what kind of car do I have?'

'What?'

'You know we took a ride down to the Paradise Cove in it? I guess I mean what kind of car did I have,' she adds rather ruefully.

'Oh yes, that car, what kind was it? I'm pretty sure it was a red one.'

'A red what?'

'A red car.'

'I mean what kind of car?'

'An old car?'

'Old! That is, or was, a vintage classic car; that was a Red 66 Mustang, you dope. At last I found your black hole, your knowledge Achilles' heel.'

Liddell however is looking thoughtful; he strokes his chin,

'Ah yes, it's coming back to me; wasn't it a Mustang Sprint 200, six-cylinder of course but with a chrome air cleaner and a special engine decal?'

'You bastard,' Costello says to him laughing at the same time. 'Come here.'

She puts her arms around him and kisses him.

Back in Liddell's room the doctor turns to Costello and kisses her again. He puts his hands between her legs; she tenses up.

'Not OK then?' he asks.

Costello sits down on the bed,

'I don't know, it's a kind of momentum thing. Back on that old rock at Santa Monica it would have been so easy, but then stopping and not being allowed sort of and all this time passing and thinking about it; I don't know.'

Liddell sits down beside her,

'We don't have to; you know I like just kissing.'

'Maybe we could make it worse by leaving it longer?'

'Why don't we try that spoons thing like in the *Frankie and Johnny* film?'

'Never saw it; what happened in it?'

'Johnny has just got out of prison; played by Al Pacino; meets Frankie who is hmm Pfeiffer and they get in bed but just cuddle up facing the same way like spoons in a drawer and don't do anything, you know, banging wise, just sort of company and closeness.'

'Yes, I think I could manage that.'

Costello pulls off her clothes and slips into the bed.

Liddell follows and she turns her back to him,

'Like this?'

He puts a tentative hand on her naked shoulder and resists the temptation to explore further,

'Exactly.'

Costello scrunches her body into his.

'This right?'

'Perfect.'

'We are a bit like the little prions you were talking about transferring shapes to one another.'

'The good ones I hope.'

'How'd you discover them?'

'I had a Creuzfeldt patient,' Liddell risks slipping his hand down to her side.

'The human form of BSE?'

'Yeh, terminal of course, I thought using an infectious protein that was opposed to the BSE ones might reverse his condition.'

'Like a gamekeeper turned poacher, I mean the other way round?'

'Kind of. He didn't survive but before he died he had some remarkably lucid memories, even including past life scenarios which we took for hallucinations of course. I wrote a paper on the whole thing which Richelieu saw and it tied in with his research into long-term memories and the good proteins. And the rest is history.'

They lie still for five minutes.

Eventually Liddell asks Costello,

'So just how did you end up in the secret service?'

She laughs; he can feel it rather than hear it,

'It's all Jodie Foster's fault; I saw a certain movie when I was just thirteen. I was hooked. Everything I did from then on, training school, exams, all with one thought in mind. When I finally got to the academy I was surrounded by about fifty young girls all with the same dream as me. You know what they called us there at the academy?'

'What?'

'The Lambs. Most dropped out.'

'I thought it was mostly guys with suits and sunglasses did that kind of job?'

'Yeh, all talking to their wrists you mean? They're not the real agents; they are called the dummies. They are like decoys; the real agents you are not meant to see.'

'Like you?'

'Yeh, exactly like me, except you and the professor didn't seem to have any problem spotting me, did you?'

'We were expecting you though.'

'So, what gave me away?'

'You were too good. Too perfect.'

'Yeh, I know, Altman 52: to err is human, fail to err and you fail ere long.'

'Altman? Is that Robert Altman, the film-maker?'

'Nah, it's short for Alternate Manual – an underground sort of bible that circulated among us lambs. The authorities didn't really approve, a little too liberal for their tastes but they never suppressed it, even they could see there was good stuff in there and a lot more accessible than their stuffy manuals which were just full of procedures and legal stuff.'

Costello scrunches up further and Liddell tries to keep the conversation going to distract himself,

'So what did you think of the last Starling book?'

'*Hannibal*?'

'Yeh, isn't that the one Jodie Foster, your hero, refused to act in because she didn't like the end where Starling goes off with Lecter?'

'I guess that's why she didn't want to do it, but they changed the end anyway in the movie, he chops…'

'Hey, don't ruin it for me, I haven't seen it.'

'Sorry. But you read the book?'

'Yes.'

'I think Jodie misunderstood; she was counting on Clarice possessing a certain loyalty to her job; sometimes though you have to be loyal to yourself.'

Another little pause and then Costello asks,

'Wait, what's that, what's going on down there?'

'Sorry I'm not really in control of my… '

'Clare and Delphi were favouring the name Willy Wonka the other day.'

'You've been talking about me and my parts with them?'

'No, not you specifically, it was more of a generic term we were discussing; but you have just given me an idea for a new topic of conversation with them for next time. I'm sure they'd have lots to say on the subject of your anatomy.'

'It would be merely hearsay.'

'Hearsay or maybe urban legend?'

There is another long pause.

'You sleeping?' Liddell finally asks.

'Yep.'

'Mind if I just explore a little?'

'I'm sleeping remember; how could I have an opinion?'

Liddell runs his hand up the inside of her leg.

'Mind if I just pop in to say goodnight?'

'I'm sleeping.'

Liddell turns her slightly and gently eases into her. Costello repeats the earlier scrunching movement until he is deep inside her.

'Goodnight,' she says softly.

Joel enters the rose garden. The President is in a hammock playing with his Game Boy. There is a familiar electronic beeping.

Joel looks over his shoulder. The President is playing Tetris, and playing rather well, Joel thinks; definitely too well for someone whose main attention should be on running the greatest nation in the world.

'You know, Joel, when you get the long thin one to go into a vertical four space, for the bonus points for clearing four lines at once, I think it is vaguely sexual. What do you think?'

'Whatever gets you through your day, sir?'

'You don't disapprove of this, do you?' asks the President holding up the still beeping toy.

'All work and no play makes the leader of the free world a dull boy, as they say.'

'Exactly, plus I'm honing my motor neurone skills for some crisis.' He switches the toy off reluctantly. 'Anyway, what's going on with all that memory business thing?'

'Well, with just a little persuasion, they have all safely relocated to New Mexico and started medicating the soldiers.' Joel looks at his papers, 'They are up to two hundred so far, doing them in batches of fifty just in case there are any adverse effects.'

'And what news?'

'As far as we can tell it appears to be working. The soldiers are all recalling past lives – no exceptions. The downside is we have done some surveys of them and it looks like the vast majority of them would be unwilling to take part in any future military action. In fact my person on the ground...'

'Not that Costello woman I hope?' interrupts the President.

'No, no, I don't think we can trust her any more. No this new guy says it is starting to look like Woodstock down there with soldiers going around with flowers in their gun barrels. Love and peace is breaking out all over.'

'Are you telling me we could end up with an army that won't fight?' the President muses, 'But on the other hand if the whole world...'

Joel dismisses the thought,

'We can't rely on that scenario, sir. What if, as is highly likely, some foreign powers refused to allow the drug to be taken in their countries; we would end up with a pansy army that would want to kiss our enemies to death.'

'I see where you're at Joel. What other developments?'

'The soldiers who have been on the course more than

three days have, without exception, all turned their backs on their religious beliefs.'

'And that could have quite an impact on my re-election campaign?'

'Certainly sir. Twenty seven percent of our funding is from the big churches. Plus some of our more aggressive foreign policies might not be so attractive to a nation bathed in brotherly love. Then there are certain secrets – military, industrial – that might start leaking out.'

The President picks one of the flowers and sniffs it tentatively,

'We let this thing go too far, Joel. We should've nipped it in the bud, back in California. What the hell can we do now?'

'Well let's look on the positive side; the good thing is that the situation is completely contained. We have total blackout in and out news wise.'

'Well that's a positive but we can't keep a thousand soldiers in there for ever. When they come out they're sure to talk, whatever we get them to sign.'

Joel leaves a little gap before the bombshell,

'I was thinking of something a little more radical sir.'

The President drops the flower,

'Joel, if you happen to be saying what I think you are, you cannot be serious; those people are our troops. They are Americans for God's sake.'

'Mr President, have I ever let you down? We need to look at the big picture,' Joel stoops down and picks up the flower, 'The greatest good for the greatest numbers; sometimes Presidents have to make hard decisions. You wouldn't think twice about sending troops in to battle if it was a matter of national security, would you?'

'Battle is one thing but this is cold blood.'

Joel decides to play his trump card.

'We have to remember that we now know we are just sending them on their way a little faster; nobody ever dies really.'

'Sometimes you scare me Joel. And you seem to have forgotten about all the Internet business. Won't we be blowing the whole thing wide open?'

'We have a little secret weapon here, sir, a certain George.'

'Don't play games with me, Joel, who the hell is George?'

'Remember a hack invasion of the pentagon a year ago – some Post-it notes left strewn all over their most secret files?'

'Oh yes – some of them were about me weren't they – pretty uncomplimentary if I remember correctly.'

'Yes, the language was a little colourful as I recall.'

'Oh yes. What happened to that son of a bitch – I hope he got seventeen years in Alcatraz.'

'Actually, sir, Alcatraz is now closed down, since sixty three actually, and the person in question would more accurately be described as a daughter of a bitch.'

'Not another one – they are taking over the whole fucking world.'

'Now, now, sir, we are in the twenty-first century. Anyway George or should we say Ms George is now working for us – better to have her inside the tent pissing out than outside pissing in..'

'Can ladies piss directionally, Joel?'

'I assure you they can, sir.'

'So you feel this DOAB can help us – where is she anyway?'

'At the moment she is living with her mother in West Virginia with a rather large security bracelet round her pretty little ankle. I'm seeing her tomorrow.'

'Give her my love.'

Joel turns to go; the President stops him,

'Oh, and about that other business, you must do what you think is right of course for the country, no need for me to be involved. You have my trust; am I clear, Joel?'

'Absolutely sir. Leave it with me.' He gives the President one of his special smiles, the one that lets the President know that all is right with the world.

Joel knocks and George's mother answers.

'Why, Joel – it's been such a long time.'

'Glad you remember me – is George home?'

'You know she is,' George's mother nods knowingly. 'You were so helpful when she got in that trouble – I don't know what we would've done without you. She hasn't been up to any more mischief has she?'

'No, no, on the contrary, your daughter is extremely talented; we think she could help us with something.'

'I'm sure she would be happy to help. She is in her room. Go ahead, you know the way.'

Joel nods and moves up the stairs. At the top of two floors he comes to a door covered with obscene graffiti, and knocks.

'Fuck off.'

'It's not your mother.'

Silence.

Joel opens the door.

'Oh it's you.'

'Hello George, glad to see you too.'

'What d'you want?'

'I thought you could help us out with a matter of national security of course.'

'Who is this us?'

'Me and the President, or should that be the President and I?'

'That creep.'

'Please don't talk about my boss like that. Anyway we have a small deal going, remember – fifteen to twenty years in a maximum-security prison with no computer access compared to your life of luxury here?'

George lays her forehead on her computer screen,

'Tell me the worst.'

Joel comes into the room and looks for an empty chair. He lifts a plate with some congealed food on it – two days old at least he calculates – from the likeliest candidate and puts it gently on the ground.

'A bad person is holding us to ransom.'

'A bad person? How old do you think I am, five?'

'I'd rather not answer that question, George. Anyway he has put up some Internet sites that contain details about how to make some prions that could infect the world. We only want you to tell us where the sites are and how to get rid of them.'

'Prions, you mean them mad cow things?'

'Exactly.'

'Is he a hacker, this guy?'

'Not really – he is a scientist – pretty brainy, doctor, maybe even a professor.'

'But is he a hacker?'

'Why do you need to know?'

'Because if he is, then you are wasting your time and mine – nobody'd find them. If I put some sites up I couldn't even find them myself.'

'No, I think he's just a smart guy.'

'Well, maybe you have a chance. What've you got for me to work on?'

'This is a clone of his hard disk.'

Joel hands over the disk and George plugs it in to one of her computers and starts rooting around inside the files,

'This might take a little time; we can't go there, or there; that's encrypted; there's a little gap here; listen Jojo, why don't you go down and chat up my mother – she's always had the hots for you. I'll give you a shout when I've got something. I work better when I ain't got some creep looking over my shoulder.'

'As you wish. By the way you already used the word creep; you really need to expand your vocabulary.'

'How about fucking creep?'

'It's a start.'

As Joel is leaving George asks him,

'Wait a minute; what's in this for me?'

'What would you like?'

'Rid of this for a start,' she gestures at the restraining anklet.

'I think it's rather becoming.'

'You ever tried taking a bath with one on?'

'Isn't it waterproof?'

'I'm not risking it. I don't want to get fried in the bath like that creep in *Doctor No*.'

'I believe you are referring to the movie *Goldfinger*. And I am afraid that much as it would like to, the government is not able to handle the publicity that would arise from all you security anklet guys getting electrocuted. I am sure it is perfectly safe in water but, OK, yes, if you are able to help us, that goes, I promise.'

Joel wanders down the stairs. George's mother is waiting anxiously at the bottom,

'I hope she wasn't rude to you.'

'She was charm personified, I assure you.'

'That is a great relief. Would you like some lemonade?'

'That would be perfect.'

Joel is drifting off in a sea of George's mother's childhood reminiscences when they hear a shout from above,

'Hey, Motherfucker!'

'That is for me I think,' Joel tells George's mother, 'and I'd guess she is referring to my mother rather than her own and not literally I assure you.'

George's mother laughs nervously,

'I don't know where she gets it from.'

Joel goes back up to George's room.

On the computer screen there are six sites underlined.

'That was quick,' Joel congratulates her, 'I thought it was going to be a lot more complicated than that.'

'Don't get too excited; these sites are dummies.'

'What do you mean by dummies, they don't work?'

'Nah, they work all right – don't send them their password everyday, which is babyjane by the way, and they spill their guts all over the Internet. Some shit about prions and memories and past lives blah blah. No they work all right.'

'So what do you mean by dummies?'

'I mean you are meant to find these. They are like decoys.'

'So there are more sites?'

'Definitely. Classically there would be three more he wouldn't want you to find but you just might. Then there would be one you wouldn't find.'

'Why just the one?'

'These things make waves – put down two and you have two waves; it's like putting all your eggs in one basket, but a very silent basket.'

'Explain?'

'Imagine the Internet is a sea, no wait a minute – where is the best place to hide a leaf?'

'In a forest.'

'And the best place to hide a body?'

'On a battlefield – I have read my Father Brown thank you.'

'Yeh, good for you, Einstein. So where do you hide some code? On – the – Internet. It's like an ocean and you are looking for some water hidden in it.'

'It sounds pretty hopeless in that case.'

'It's tricky all right; but you've come to the right place; listen, you put your toe in a pond it makes ripples no matter how gently you put it in. There are always ripples, always.'

'So you can find them, the three sites and the one invisible one?'

'I can definitely get you the three – might take a week, but the one? There is something strange about these codes, even the easy ones; they're weird.'

'What do you mean weird?'

'They are not like any codes I seen before. What does he do this guy?'

'This stuff with prions and proteins.'

'It's not on the net anywhere. I had a quick look.'

'They took it down, but I can get you his research.'

'Might help.'

As Joel is leaving George fires a parting shot,

'Wait, there is this company makes little bagel shaped crackers I like.'

'And?'

'And they gone out of business.'

'And you want me to start them up again just like that?'

'National security, remember.'

'I'll see what I can do,' Joel sighs.

Liddell and Richelieu have roped in Costello to go through the memory books of the soldiers. The doctors are concentrating on the health checks – so far not too bad, one breakdown, and seven migraines that responded well to conventional treatment. Out of three hundred soldiers so far this is not worrying.

Costello goes through the books feeding the statistics into her laptop. They are ignoring current memories and concentrating on verifiable facts of past lives for the minute. First off, all the global distribution is roughly following the population figures, a few bumps here and there – quite a lot of eastern Europeans but nothing outside natural statistical averages. The male to female balance is also nicely reflecting global norms and is, as predicted, completely irrespective of the current sex of the soldiers. Just from hanging around the canteen Costello can feel the buzz that is arising from this. There is a subtle transformation of the dominant macho nature of the soldiers and not just the male soldiers either. She also remembers the question about population growth that Brewer had asked; Liddell seemed to think that maybe one in a hundred would have no past but so far this doesn't seem to be the case; she makes a note to ask him.

Next she inputs the latest data on previous names, addresses and birthdates. These are going off to an army of checkers worldwide who are tracking down the names and then finding as much about them for immediate checking. The American and European confirmations are coming back almost by return. The African and Far East seem much harder to trace. Everything that comes back is positive though.

Costello has sneakily snuck in her own Xhosa name but nothing is back on that so far; she guesses it is not just a case of going to the local birth/death registry down there. Costello takes a certain pleasure in the recognition of the soldiers' current names and imagining the various personalities coming to terms with the pairings of past lives she is copying down – some links are perfect whereas others are downright perverse.

Richelieu comes in; Costello can tell from the colour of his face how mad he is, today between mauve and beetroot, not good. He is waving some form,

'The soldiers have been told to fill these in, and not for us.'

Costello looks at the piece of paper; it is a series of detailed questions with tick boxes. She scans it quickly, and a few of the questions jump out at her, 'Would you be prepared to kill?' questions on sexuality, nationality...

'I knew nothing of this.'

'You are out of their loop I'd say, Costello. As far as they are concerned you are now one of us.'

'Let me phone Joel. Also me and Liddell are meeting groups one and two this afternoon; we can ask them about all this.'

Costello goes to the only phone in the camp. It is in an office with an armed guard. Costello remembers how Sylvie, Clare and Delphi had to be wrestled to the ground to give up their phones. Their cell phones were part of their anatomy. She gives the special code to the operator on the line and is quickly through to Joel.

'How's it going in there?'

'Well the food's not so great.'

'You should see how bad it is at the White House.'

'Yeh I can imagine, all that rich stuff, creams and sauces; you must get so sick of it and long for some stewed mess hall cabbage.'

'My mouth is watering already, Costello. Why are you ringing, some problem?'

'Soldiers have been asked to fill in a questionnaire. Nothing to do with our tests; we weren't even told.'

'Oh that, don't worry, it's a standard issue form, every soldier in the country has been filling them in.'

Costello thinks Joel is probably lying here but she has no way of checking up on it. She carries on,

'I don't think you need to be worried; this is a great step forward for humanity. So I'm guessing your soldiers might lose a little of their keen-ness to kill other people, but is that really so bad after all?'

'Don't misunderstand us, Costello, the President and I

are both very excited by your progress down there. We are already thinking of the next steps, with larger tests and how to proceed after that.'

'Perhaps if you came down and talked to the soldiers in person you'd get more of a perspective.'

'Well I am already tempted by the cabbage; difficult for me to get away at present; these are busy times; we also have a President to get re-elected. I will check my schedules. Take care.'

Liddell and Costello enter the mess hall. It is the first time they have seen Group One all together since the initial meeting. Costello knows that the mood is generally good among the volunteers but is taken aback when they stand up and applaud en masse on their entry.

'Well what's going on?' she shouts over the noise.

Staff Sergeant Grant quietens them all down. He puts his hands together and says solemnly,

'This is the dawning of a new age.'

The rest of the room nods, not exactly gravely, but seriously. Costello cannot believe the difference in the room from their first meeting. Gone is the boisterous competitiveness, replaced with the deep sense of warmth and confidence she remembered from the original patients at Santa Monica. But in their case she had never met them before their treatment so the change was not so apparent, or dramatic. Twice as much experience, twice as much love and suffering. In fact more than that, most of these soldiers were in their twenties and now had the whole experience of maybe sixty year olds as well, making a total of more like four times the experience.

Liddell answers,

'We are touched by your appreciation. We thought it would be a good thing for you to share your past life experiences with each other and us of course. Who would like to start?'

One by one, each soldier stands. As predicted they are all remembering unexceptional lives, but yet to them these lives are entirely exceptional. Many cry as they describe families and friends. Particularly moving is how half of them can describe their own deaths. Costello guesses the others died in their sleep or maybe suddenly with no warning. Some of the deaths are painful, some lingering, some surrounded by loved ones, some terribly alone, but even those last seem transfigured by what has now happened. Costello decides to join in and tells of her life as Themba. She too is overcome and Liddell gently puts his arm around her shoulders.

On the way out Costello says to Liddell,

'Richelieu should've been here. He needs to hear all this stuff.'

'Richelieu is a scientist. He needs to be objective, all this emoting merely muddies the water in his eyes.'

'This isn't science any more. You heard them. This is everything; politics, religion, family, the whole of life.'

The two of them go to the Japanese garden Joe has built. Costello has no idea how Joe persuaded the flint faced commander of the camp to give him the space and permission but he had no trouble in recruiting some helpers to build it. The place is small but with its big stones and raked gravel it has an aura of serenity. They sit on one of the boulders.

'I've been wondering. How does it work?' Costello asks.

'You mean the memory transfer thing?'

'Yeh, the whole business of how the memories actually get

from one person to another. Where do they go in between? What are memories without a person or a brain anyway?'

'I was wondering when you'd ask.'

'Well?'

'Not a clue. Not even a hypothesis really. We call them the big three questions, me and Richy; why, how and what happens in between.'

'But you must've speculated, that's what you scientists do.'

'Of course.'

'And?'

'Well Richelieu favours some kind of matrix of memory, a sort of holistic thing. Possibly involving everybody's memories.'

'And you?'

'Me? I'm going more for another dimension kind of thing.'

'Like what?'

'Like where your real consciousness resides and just the tip of it is in our world.'

'So when you die it kind of ducks down back into the,' here Costello does a scary voice, 'fourth dimension and then pops back up when you get reborn.'

'Have you got a better idea?' Liddell says defensively.

'Sounds pretty far fetched to be honest.'

'Well not really any more than the whole weirdness of consciousness itself. Nobody has a clue about that, the fact that the whole universe is in your head like in that Dickinson poem. How does that happen?'

'But if there was this matrix hanging around, or things popping from other dimensions, wouldn't you be able to notice it with all your scientific gizmos and everything?'

'We only know what we know, if you had explained to

Isaac Newton what radio waves were he would have thought you were crazy; there's tons of stuff we know nothing about and that's just the stuff we know we know nothing about as opposed to…'

'Old Rumsfeld's unknown unknowns? Whatever happened to him?'

A week after his first visit Joel rings the bell at George's mother's house. No response, he tries again twice. Still no answer. Well George has to be home, he knows that at least, unless the little bastard has found some way to trick the security anklet. He hammers on the door and shouts through the letterbox. Eventually George opens a window high up at the top of the house and shouts down,

'It's open dickhead.'

Joel sighs and goes in and up the stairs.

George is staring at her computer screens,

'Twice in one month, you got the hots for me, Billy Joel?'

'In your dreams, and if you call me Billy Joel again I will personally reconsider your prison sentence.'

'Now, now. Remember our mission.'

Joel sits down,

'Anyway, here are your bagel crackers.'

He throws over a pack and George starts munching immediately. The way that George eats reminds Joel of someone and he makes a mental note to present the President with a packet of the bagel crackers next time they meet,

'You said you had a breakthrough?'

'First, though, I been reading the shit on his Internet sites.

Looks like he's made up something that lets you know what your past lives were. Sounds pretty cool, I'd like to try that myself.'

'You believe everything you see on the Internet? That's just a trick, it's simply a device to get people taking his poison.'

'So what is it then?'

'Pretty much like the old mad cow stuff but with a longer incubation period and much more infectious among humans.'

George muses for a while,

'So some dopes read this, then make these things, then take them to get their past lives?'

'Exactly, and by the time they realise it doesn't work he's already infected enough people to spread it right round the world.'

'Excellent, it's just like in that *Twelve Monkeys* movie.'

'If you like.'

'So why doesn't he just blast it out there now. Why all this dicking around with these sites and all?'

'He's blackmailing us of course, wants a lot of money to not release the information.'

'You know, I like the sound of this guy. He's extra cool. I'm on his side, wouldn't be so bad a planet without humans, all the animals running all over the place.'

'No, humans includes you and your mom. Both dying horrible painful slow deaths. This is your chance to be a superhero – George saves the world.'

'But the world will never know.'

'Me and the President will know and we will be very grateful.'

George thinks about posterity for a while and then,

'Sure, let's do it, maybe some day I'll be in a movie!'

'Yeh maybe, so what you got?'

'Only got just the three we weren't supposed to find,' says George proudly. 'Secret was in the way he folds up his code. It's pretty neat like origami stuff. I can use some of his ideas in future. Trouble for him is it's kind of distinctive so I been trawling for four days and look what I fished up.' George brings up three addresses.

'Let's take a look.'

'No, no, no, we do that and he will know we looked.'

'But you looked at the other six already.'

'He meant us to find them remember – if we hadn't found them and looked at them he would probably have thought something was up.'

'So how do you disable these three without going into them?'

'We leave them there and we snip the links that attach to them. If nobody can get to them then they are dead in the water.'

'How do you know it'll work?'

'Remember when the doors to Aircraft One wouldn't open for two days in Jakarta.'

'Course I remember, I was on that plane you little fuck.'

'I know, I can still hear you squealing about bombs. Get us off, get us off!'

'They had to cut us out of that plane in the end. So that was you?'

'Sure, want me to do it again?'

'No, but give me details how you did it and then I'll believe you can do this.'

George picks up a disk,

'It's all already on this here plus a little virus to let loose.

There's a blank space to put in the final address when I get it for you. Then you just press the button marked disappear. Think you can manage that?' George tosses the disk on the floor, 'Now you disappear. I gotta find your last missing link.'

Joel picks up the disk,

'It'd better be soon,' he says as he leaves.

After Joel is gone George opens up the sixth of Liddell's high visibility sites. She posts a little note to be sent when it is pinged.

Hi Liddell

Looks like me and you got a lot in common

By the way you are being watched.

I can help – you can get me at

Ghostxx@hotmail.com

George plays around with the colour of the note for a while. Eventually she decides on baby blue.

Costello looks at Liddell lying asleep. She has to tell him. She shakes him gently.

'What time is it?' he asks.

'I cloned your computer.'

'What, just now?'

'No, back in Santa Monica, back at the clinic.'

'Why?'

'Part of my job.'

'When? I never let it out of my sight?'

'When you were looking for the Bachman Warbler.'

'You know about birds?'

'Nope. I know about that extinct warbler only. I had to distract you so I could copy your data.'

'So you didn't see one after all?'

Costello is not sure whether he is more upset about the bird or the computer.

'No.'

'Shame, well I thought it would have been lost in the fire anyway. The clone, you sent it off to your Joel?'

'Yep, that very same afternoon.'

'It was mostly encrypted stuff. Do you think they could get into it?'

'What level was it?'

'256.'

'Should be safe, at least for a couple of years.'

'Was there anything else you did you want to tell me about?'

'Richelieu's computer first day I arrived.'

'Silly old fool, nothing on it I expect. You know what his password is?'

'Yep, France.'

They both laugh.

'Also I sent off the first pills you gave me, the ones I didn't take. Do you think they could synthesize them?'

'Who knows? Well it will all soon be academic. In two weeks we finish these initial tests and as everything has gone smoothly including all the safety checks, they have no excuse not to go onto the larger more public versions. So we would need to scale up production of the prions anyway.'

'Soon you're going to need billions of your little pills,' Costello sits astride Liddell.

'But do you still love me?'

'Because of the computer thing? Promise you won't do it again?'

'I promise.'

'OK, I still love you. Let's go get some delicious breakfast.'

Costello jumps off,

'You know, I'm not so sure those pills don't make you delusional.'

On their way to the mess hall Costello asks Liddell about the fact that they still haven't found anyone without a past memory although there should not be enough to go around.

'That issue was bothering me even before we got this information,' he answers.

'How come?'

'Well if the memory kick starts our learning processes, say with evolutionary advantages, how would that be for people without it?'

'I see where you are coming from. Any theories in there?' she says tapping Liddell's head.

'Of course,' he laughs. 'We don't know that everyone gets a unique life; two people might get the same one. We would only know if we were doing millions of tests.'

'Like somebody else could have gotten my Themba?' Costello suddenly feels very protective. 'That's not fair.'

'Well it's only a hundred to one. But if we go far back there used to only be a million people around so maybe the memories divide like amoebae.'

'I don't get it. You saying after I die I could go into two different people, which one would I be for God's sake?'

Liddell laughs,

'Who are you now? Take a thought experiment, say in the

future we could scan you in some way and then build a new you molecule by molecule, an exact duplicate.'

'Like a clone?'

'No a clone isn't an exact copy, by the time it grows up it has completely different memories, and past memories for that matter. No this is an exact copy, every atom. Say we could do that with some tiny nanobots, which one would you be?'

Costello is facing brain overload and is glad to see Janeway and two of her friends coming out of the camp headquarters,

'What's up?' Costello asks her.

'We've just been to see the Commandant to talk about discharges – not immediately, only once your experiment is over of course.'

'What all three of you?'

'No, not only us, we're just a delegation, for nearly the whole camp. Eight-hundred and seventy-three want to leave. Only sixty-two want to stay. They believe the army needs them at least transitionally.'

'What did he say?'

'Nothing he can, really, we got the usual speech about serving our nation, how it was one of the noblest professions, sacrifice blah. Maybe we should slip him some of your pills in his coffee?'

The three go back to break the news to their colleagues.

Costello looks after them,

'Well looks like we have started destroying the Army.'

'Good thing too. I'm hopeful that a lot of the shit things in the world will disappear.'

'Like what?'

'Male domination and organised religion for a start.'

'You religious, you know before all this?' Costello asks.

Liddell lets out a puff of air.

'I was officially Church of Scotland, Protestant, but my parents never went to church except to funerals and the odd wedding.'

'No, I didn't mean were you a church goer, I meant what did you believe in?'

'Well putting my old scientist's head back on I find it impossible to believe anything. I can only speculate. Nothing is ever provable you know.'

'Some things are.'

'Like what?'

'Like, well, for example, the fact that we are here, now.'

'Not necessarily, this could be an illusion, or a dream I'm having, or you are having, or somebody else is having.'

Costello pinches him on the arm rather viciously,

'You dreaming now?'

Liddell rubs his arm,

'Careful, that doesn't prove anything, you can get pinched in a dream and also feel pain. But in any case this might be an especially vivid, real dream, our whole lives long.'

'If nothing is believable what's the point of anything?'

'Well that's what I said. Let's speculate, for example, I think you might just be there, or even if you are not, I like talking, and doing other things to whatever I imagine you might be, whether you're real or a dream, so I do that.'

'So if you had died and gone to heaven and met God you would still be going hmm rather interesting but you might not really be there?'

'Exactly, nothing could convince me that even in that case

everything might not still change in an instant.'

'So getting back to religion what did you speculate before all this past lives business started?'

'I thought that there was probably round about a sixty percent chance that we just popped into the world, lived our lives and at the end died and then nothingness, end of story.'

'Fair enough.'

'Twenty percent that life was some kind of illusion, a dream or maybe some elaborate video type game. Another ten percent that after death we carried on in some other way like reincarnation. And I left nine point nine percent for something we have not even thought about.'

'That old unknown unknown again?'

'Yes.'

'And all those old religions, Christianity and Islam, Judaism?'

'I popped them into the zero point one percent probability.'

'They are not going to be too happy all squashed up together like that in such a tiny space.'

'No, I don't expect so and the sun worshippers and spaghetti monster believers are in there with them too.'

'By sun worshipers I take it you mean people that actually praise the sun rather than just those people that like to fry on beaches?'

'Yep, like druids. The beach friers are dopes one step up from cigarette smokers.'

'So Venice Beach must have been quite a blast the first time you saw it. Anyway what has changed now in your speculations with this prion stuff?'

'Not too much, just a swapping of the reincarnation probability with the end of everything possibility.'

'Surely that is not possible for both of them to be true?'

'Not possible is not a phrase we can use, remember? For all we know we could reincarnate a few times and then pfft, that's all folks.'

'But it's not so likely now, I mean in the Liddell sweepstakes?'

'Yeh I put that end of everything possibility down to ten percent, bumped up the reincarnation thing to seventy. The reason why I had the nothingness thing so high before was that there was no obvious mechanism how thoughts and memories could be transferred after death.'

'But you said the other day that you still don't know how that happens.'

'Yes, we don't know how but at least now we know that it does happen.'

Costello is thoughtful for a while, then,

'I guess the big western religions will go?'

'Certainly they won't survive as they are. They will be hit on three sides.'

'Which are?'

'Firstly they will have to do some explaining as to why none of them promote earthly re-incarnation – I think they initially might get around that with a load of revisionary adjustments, after all they do all have small sects that believe in it. The second wave to hit them will be from the population getting wiser, more tolerant, less sexist, less happy to put up with their manipulations.'

'And the third from not having that old fear of death to entice people in?' Costello suggests.

'Yes, that should be the final nail in their coffin, and no bad thing, they were never about spirituality or religion in the first place but mere political, male-dominated systems bent on control. The first global superpowers really.'

'I guess there will be some winners like Hinduism and Tibetan Buddhism?'

'I think even that would be temporary. They will get an initial boost but eventually it will trickle through that a lot of what they say doesn't really tie in with what we have discovered. Truth will out in the end.'

'Yeh, and that reminds me I have to find Joe. Today is confessions day,' Costello admits unenthusiastically.

Joe is in his Japanese garden reading.

'Joe,' Costello says.

He jumps.

'Sorry, I didn't mean to frighten you. I hate when people do that to me.'

Joe nods and pats the boulder next to him and Costello sits down and takes a deep breath,

'Remember you told me those names and stuff before? I found out who they are.'

'How come? I thought the camp was closed, sealed up. No information in or out at all?'

'It is, but I found out when you first told me, back at your dad's place.'

'Why didn't you tell me then?'

'It's a long story. Anyway, you want to hear what I found out?'

'Sure, but a lot has become clearer to me since then anyway.' Joe closes his book.

'In a previous life you were Tanganyika, and you lived in north Japan in that village.'

'Senso.'

'Yep.'

'And I know now who the others were.'

'You do?'

'Yes, Seera was my wife and Hano and Miko were my two children.'

'I guess they still are your children in a way.'

'You know where they are living?'

'Yep, Hano is still in your village, Senso, and Miko is at Tokyo university studying literature. Doing quite well apparently.'

Costello leaves a little pause.

Joe looks at her anxiously,

'And Seera?'

Costello puts her arm around him,

'Killed herself seven months after you died.'

'Because of me?'

'It looks like it. She did it at your graveside apparently.'

There are tears in Joe's eyes,

'But if this reincarnation thing is happening to everybody then that means she is probably around now and about my age again?'

'It would seem likely.'

'I have to find her.'

'Hang on a minute Joe, how can you do that?'

Joe pushes her arm away and stands up,

'Well we know she must have been born say a year after she died.'

'Do you happen to know how many people are born in the world every year; we don't even know if she is a man or a woman?'

'I wouldn't care which she was. I love her whatever. And

doesn't it seem that she loves me as much?'

'It looks like she did, Joe, but she doesn't remember all that. More than a hundred million people must have been born that year. It would be like looking for a needle in a haystack except that it's not even a needle, it's a stalk of hay in a haystack the size of LA. And even if you picked up the right stalk you still wouldn't know it was the right one, even if it was in your hand. You might already have bumped into her without realising.'

'We'd know each other if we met.'

'She could be in China, Africa, anywhere.'

'But if we give the drugs to everybody in the world then she would remember me too and then it would be easy, with the Internet, friends reunited and all that stuff. My father could help, he could get the prions made cheaply enough for everybody.'

'Well steady on. That is possibly part of the bigger plan, but we have to make sure they are safe, more trials, before we give them to the whole world. You need to be patient.'

'When you meet with her you will understand why that is so hard.'

'I'm sure I will Joe, I'm sure I will.'

Costello finds Liddell at a table outside the mess hall. He has a couple of pancakes and a coke.

Costello holds the bottle between two fingers and waves it slightly,

'Wouldnt've thought this was your drink of choice?'

'Just trying to blend in. The American dream.'

She puts the bottle back and sits down with a long sigh.

'What's up?' Liddell asks.

'I just told Joe that his wife in his previous life killed herself.'

'How on earth did you know that?'

'Joe asked me to find out about some names he was remembering and Joel tracked the three of them down in Japan back when we were at Santa Monica. They were his two kids and his wife who committed suicide at his grave.'

'That's tough. How did Joe take it?'

'He wants to find her of course.'

'And you explained just how tricky that might be?'

'Tried to, but it's got me thinking, what if we do go global with this, what will happen to all those people in relationships when they discover their previous husbands wives and lovers are around. Won't it destroy them, the current relationships, mess up their happy lives?'

Liddell cuts his pancakes in two and offers half to Costello,

'Not necessarily, people are already dealing with multiple relationships in their lives now. It's a rare person these days who only has one important significant other in their whole life. I guess some relationships from the past like Joe's might be strong enough to reassert themselves but my guess is that would not be the majority. Maybe a new way of looking at relationships might evolve anyway. People are resilient.'

'The words 'worms' and 'can' keep springing to my mind these days.'

'I think the words Pandora and Box are more relevant, at least you can get the worms back in the can.'

'So?'

'So the box is already open and can't be closed. When this lot go home and start spreading the word nearly everybody is going to want to try it. And if we can make sure it's as safe as possible then we shouldn't stop them. It's a matter of free will. Nobody so far has regretted it and if it breaks up a few relationships well that's happening anyway every day of the week. Plus just think how it will change world poverty for example; say you are a rich person you could be dead in an hour and in a year back in some family that is starving; that should be some incentive to people to level things out.'

Costello nods,

'I guess you're right, but it's so strange knowing something that all the rest of the world doesn't know yet, but soon will.'

'How do you think me and Richelieu felt at the start? Anyway I better ping the websites or it will be all over the world. Back in five minutes.'

Liddell goes off to the central office and Costello toys with the pancakes.

Five minutes later he comes back looking concerned.

Costello notices,

'What's up?'

'When I pinged one of the sites this came back.'

Liddell has written George's message on the back of his hand. Costello reads it carefully,

'So someone has discovered your sites?'

'This was one of the ones that was meant to be discoverable, if you were looking. The information there is still encrypted unless it doesn't get the ping so it means the information about folding the prions is still secret.'

'So who wrote this message?'

'Maybe Joel?'

'It doesn't sound like him.'

'What if it is maybe Joel trying not to sound like himself?'

'He is devious but he just couldn't put that together, it's too, too…'

'Chavy?'

'What?'

'Oh I forgot you don't speak English, well trailer trashy?'

'Yeh. Maybe it's someone who is working for him but who really is on your side?'

'That's possible.'

'What are you going to do about it?'

'I think it is best we do nothing, the tests are underway, the genie is out of the bottle, and the sites are still safe as far as I know. We knew they would be watching and looking, why they wouldn't be doing their jobs if they weren't.'

The three-week anniversary in the camp is celebrated by a big basketball game, KARC versus the US Military. For the previous week Lippi has been training the gang and has finally chosen his team of five – he has negotiated a two substitutes limit pointing out the slightly biased odds of the playing pool, that is to say a thousand to ten – eventually USM agrees to limit the opposing team to members of the Group One test subjects. Costello has significantly improved her ball skills and as the only one of the bunch apart from Lippi that could be described as fit has been designated Power Forward. Liddell in view of his height is Centre. Clare in view of her extreme beauty will be used to distract the opposition as Shooting Guard and Maybel is designated Small Forward. Lippi of course is Point Guard and on-court coach.

Lippi has been spying on the opposition in training and gives his assessment; Brewer has height on his side but wears glasses; Lewis is fast but undisciplined; Greys looks harmless but has great ball skills. On balance the army team is much fitter but KARC has a secret weapon, himself.

The first two quarters go fairly even, but KARC falls behind in the third; partly due to Maybel stuffing the ball under her jersey and shouting 'Pregnant woman coming through!' Everyone stops in amazement and her perfect hoop is immediately disqualified and three penalty throws awarded to the opposition.

In the end, despite a magnificent final throw by Lippi from practically the opposite end of the court, which brings the house down, KARC loses by two points.

Lippi maintains they really had won as he considered the penalties for Maybel's stunt were too harsh as it was an obvious Globetrotters moment rather than a deliberate attempt to cheat and takes them all to the bar for a celebratory drink.

The whole eleven of them squash around a table, even Hendrix the nurse and surprisingly Richelieu, sporting shorts and sunglasses. Costello wonders if he has started taking the prions but Liddell assures her not.

Holding his glass high Lippi declares,

'There is only one word suitable to describe this team, unique.'

'Wait,' says Delphi, 'If some virus or something knocked all the words out everybody's heads in the whole world except just one essential word, what should that one be? Come on, quick fire answer, no thinking.' She points at everybody on the table one by one, 'Now quick.'

'Kiss,' from Liddell.

'Sap,' Delphi comments.

'Help,' from Maybel.

'Useful.'

'Love,' Little Joe.

'Aw, sweet.'

'Croissant,' from Richelieu.

'Mmm.'

'No,' from Clare.

'Ah one for the ladies.'

'Yes,' Lippi

'One for the boys.'

'Home,' Hendrix.

'Family,' Costello.

'Drink,' Sylvie

'None,' says Markus.

'Do you mean the word for a religious lady who wears a habit or the word none or actually no words at all?'

'No word at all; if we've gone that far might as well go the whole hog,' Markus confirms.

'What about you Delphi, we told you ours?' asks Sylvie.

'Mine would have to be fuck,' answers Delphi. 'You get two meanings out of it; as a useful swear word and also a verb, without which,' she raises her glass, 'none of us would be here.'

Liddell and Costello slip out of the bar, it is already twilight.

Costello puts her arm through Liddell's,

'They're taking it well but it is a bit strange to be cooped up in here without knowing what's going on out there in the real world.'

'Who knows what could be happening?' Liddell agrees.

'Well why don't I go and get us a paper; there is a little town just five miles away, to the south?'

'What are you going to do, just walk out the front gate.

The place is swarming with armed soldiers remember, and ones who still love their jobs and country.'

'I'll slip out the back way. Don't forget I'm trained for this kind of thing. Anyway, they're expecting to keep people out, not to keep people in here from escaping. Plus I have my bush skills, I could probably smell a soldier two hundred metres downwind.'

'That's not bush skills, anybody can do that.' Both laugh.

Costello pick up a few things from her hut and puts on her darkest clothes. She comes back out to the waiting Liddell who kisses her and then asks,

'And get me a coffee while you are out there, a real coffee.'

'Sure thing, anything else?'

'Yes, you take care of yourself.'

'Don't worry your pretty little head. I'll only be gone away a couple of hours.'

Liddell closes his eyes and recites,

'Remember me when I am gone away,'

Costello stops in the doorway,

'What's that?'

'First line of a poem.'

'How does it go on?'

'Remember me when I am gone away,
Gone far away into the silent land;
When you can no more hold me by the hand,
Nor I half turn to go, yet turning stay.
Remember me when no more day by day
You tell me of our future that you plann'd:'

Liddell creases his forehead, 'That's all I can remember.'

Costello comes back and kisses him,

'It's beautiful, sad but beautiful, hey, try and remember

the rest by the time I get back.'

Liddell nods and repeats,

'And take care of yourself.'

'You already said that.'

Costello slips behind one of the barrack sheds and creeps up to the electrified fence. She takes out a set of wires with little clips on them and attaches them to the wires of the fence on either side of her. Then with a pair of pliers neatly snips the wires between. She eases herself through the gap and into the scrub behind the camp.

She takes a deep breath. It is the same air she was breathing two minutes before but it feels different. She then heads south skirting the camp, running with a low lolloping stride unfamiliar to her legs.

Joel sits by the hotel phone, a little nervous but also rather excited. It feels a bit like the scene at the end of that *Godfather* film where everything is finally sorted out in a synchronised ballet – all the loose ends cauterised, payback time.

First he gets a call from the invisible man in Durham. Chloroform to knock them out that will evaporate in the succeeding house fire. No problem, no evidence; just a cursory glance by the fire chief at the amount of computers running from one power line on the top floor should convince him the house was a virtual death trap. Joel feels a slight pang of regret for George's mother but none for the little brat. He gives the go-ahead.

Next the big one. The tough decision had been whether to be around to manage the fallout (ha-ha) or to keep a discrete distance. His final decision was to let it blow over and then move in a few days later to clean up. This time the voice on the phone call says only the three words 'yes or no.' After the slightest of hesitations Joel quietly says,

'Yes.'

Lastly the viruses or is it Trojans; whatever. He slips George's disk into the drive. George has named the programme ironically Die Sucker. At first Joel had thought it was German – the sugar? Joel carefully types in the final address that George had emailed him into the waiting space and then double clicks on the word disappear and a little graphic hoodie guy reminiscent of South Park comes up with the ten sites ranged as other little cartoon characters on little gibbets, six little ones, three medium ones and one large one. One by one the hoodie guy points and squeaks 'die sucker' and they are executed. Then once they are all done a little jolly tune and a Bugs Bunny 'that's all folks' pops up. Joel quickly removes the disk from his computer; never know what else the little bastard might have put on it.

Then he gets a coke and switches on the TV. He jumps from world news to CNN to BBC. All are leading at the moment with their own small stories, a crash here, a flood there, small beer. He gains a certain satisfaction from knowing that in less than half an hour they will have forgotten those stories and will be jumping around like rabbits trying to find their maps of New Mexico and contacting their professors of nuclear radiation and at the moment only he and maybe three other people know this knowledge that tomorrow will be on the tips of the whole world's tongues. That's power.

He takes a sip from the bottle and says to the waiting TV,

'Bring it on.'

The air is cooling as Costello reaches the outskirts of the little town in less than thirty minutes. She stops briefly to take it in; adjusts her clothing a little and then walks into the town. At first she can't put her finger on what is wrong; suddenly it hits her, no sound, no people, no nothing. A ghost town. But then again not a ghost town, the place is clean, well kept; it's more of a Marie Celeste town. She checks her watch; it is still only 9.30. Half way down Main Street she sees a light in a shop down a side road. A liquor store. She heads down and peers in the window. Just some old guy sitting at the counter with a shotgun.

Well maybe not such a bad idea, get Liddell some whisky instead of the coffee. She goes in.

'Hi,' she says to the old guy.

He doesn't answer.

'Can I get a bottle of Black Label?' she points to the bottle behind his head. He reaches back without taking his eyes off her and puts it on the counter.

'Fourteen dollars.'

She puts the money on the counter and asks casually,

'Say, where is everybody?'

'You not from here?'

'Just passing through.'

'Heard there was road blocks all around the town?'

'Must've missed them. You didn't say where all the people are?'

'Evacuated. The lot of them. I wouldn't go. Last time I went, cause of some hurricane, got back and the store was trashed, and not by the storm neither.'

'Why was everybody evacuated this time, another storm on its way?'

'Nah, some kind of terrorist threat up at the army base.'

A coldness comes over Costello,

'What kind of threat was it?'

'Didn't say, didn't say much at all, but it must be big one, that place is more than five miles away from here.'

'When did it happen, the evacuation?'

'This morning. Most people were still in bed, came through with loudhailers, scared the shit out of everybody, was like the end of the world, like in one of them movies.'

Costello turns to the door and pulls it open.

'Wait, you forgot your whisky,' he calls out after her but she is already halfway up the side street. She turns up Main Street now sprinting. She leaves the town on the highway, running up the middle of the deserted road. Her breath is now burning her lungs.

Two miles up the road although she is running with her eyes closed she sees a sheet of white light. Blinded she stumbles on, her momentum carrying her forward. Then a long, long pause before a wind and a howling. She throws herself down onto the road as the wave of heat and dust and debris flow over her. Then as suddenly as the furore started there is absolute silence.

She rolls herself over into the ditch at the edge of the road and pulls some leaves over herself. The rescue teams would be here soon but not looking for survivors. What was the last thing he said to her? Take care of yourself. She starts crying.

EPILOGUE

Costello guns through the bush in the old pickup jeep she had bought in Johannesburg. The eleven months since the explosion have seen her using every single one of her many skills and a few that she didn't know she had. The initial escape from the area had been pretty straightforward, well who was looking for survivors from that mini holocaust? But then again she couldn't be sure that they wouldn't eventually be looking for her. Nuclear forensics, what was that like these days? How much would be left of everybody to test who they had been? Would they sift through the dust in their white suits trying to identify blackened stumps or would they simply cover the place in concrete as quickly as possible? She couldn't take the risk as she was probably the only living innocent witness of a massive crime, what would it be? Battallioncide? She worries briefly about the old guy in the liquor store, would he be questioned, remember her, identify her? There had been nothing to connect her with the camp apart from her flight from the shop.

At around three in the morning, wearing just shorts, t-shirt and sneakers, with hardly any money and no way of accessing any of her funds without setting off alarm bells, she headed back to the deserted town, helicopters whirring overhead. The empty town proved easy pickings for her. Selecting an expensive looking house – they could afford to lose some stuff – she was in in minutes. New clothes, not exactly her style. Some money. She started vomiting and couldn't tell if it was radiation sickness or just shock and distress. A bath? She started crying again in the bath and couldn't stop. She has really only stopped crying a year later when she got to this beautiful country, home.

She pulls the map out of the bag, driving with one hand, still not in familiar territory. She pats the little bag of the last of her precious pills on the passenger seat.

The trip back to Santa Monica had been traumatic. But her memories were fading fast. She tried to shift as many of them from their temporary holding place into permanent areas, repeating names and information, writing everything down, but the language especially without somebody to speak to was slipping away fast. She needed the prions. The burnt out mansion hadn't really been touched and once she had located the pharmacy it was fairly easy to dig down and find the safe with the medicines in it. Even found herself a little two inch curl of a Kandinsky as she was leaving, wondering if it was worth anything.

She switches on the radio. Some singing – it is a livecast from a memorial service from some big church in New York. The hymn finishes and that old familiar voice of the President, the newly re-elected President, comes on. He pays tribute to the good soldiers who died in that terrible terrorist nuclear attack a year ago, a little hesitation betraying some deep but controlled emotional wells, why maybe there is even a tear in his eye. He regains control and his voice firms stalwartly as he tells the waiting nation that they have at last analysed the atomic signature of the plutonium in the bomb. They know which country it originated from and are already preparing for military action against them. Costello switches off the radio before he can call down God's blessing on her and her fellow countrymen. She turns a corner and at last recognises some familiar landmarks. She throws the map into the back and accelerates.

After the memorial service Joel is sitting in the back of his limo. He had slipped out the side door as usual. Let them photograph the puppets, not the master. The big car starts on the drive back down to Washington – Joel has been nervous of flying ever since the Jakarta thing. Of course little George is no more, or at least she or he is not called George probably and not any trouble for at least ten years, precocious little bastard, but Joel knows there is an army of other Georges just as clever, if not more so, out there. They had caught George after all. If it is that easy to lock the doors of a plane on the other side of the world then it must be as easy to open them mid-Atlantic. Joel shudders; he pours himself some sparkling water and switches on some Vivaldi. He takes out a little bottle of pills and spills some onto his hand. He holds one up to the light as if the little white crystalline form would somehow tell him something. 'Not easy to make,' his chemist had said. Joel had asked, 'Are you sure it's exactly the same as the original, not just the molecules but the way it is folded?' Patiently the chemist showed him some blowups of both the molecules. 'Trust me these are the same.'

Joel puts the tablet with the others and shuffles them back into the bottle. He is not worried about the safety of the pills themselves, no he is worried about the person he might meet from beyond the grave – or rather from beyond the womb. Maybe he is not so much worried what he will think of that person but more what that one will think of him. He puts the bottle back in his pocket – maybe tomorrow.

Costello turns off the road and onto little more than a track through the scrub and stops for a little break. She is so near – maybe she wants to savour the moment of return or maybe she is just a little bit scared of what she will find. Out loud she speaks the second half of the poem that Liddell couldn't quite recall but she has long since memorised,

'Only remember me; you understand
It will be late to counsel then or pray.
Yet if you should forget me for a while
And afterwards remember, do not grieve:
For if the darkness and corruption leave
A vestige of the thoughts that once I had,
Better by far you should forget and smile
Than that you should remember and be sad.'

She smiles.

Strange how the silent land where Liddell has gone is actually this noisy world itself. The silence is that tiny barrier of knowing, or not knowing rather; a few little folded molecules are all that lie between them. As Richelieu had so astutely said, 'If one person takes the prions then they can go back in time whereas if everybody takes them we can all go boldly into the future.'

She wonders where the little Eric is or maybe it really is Lydia now, mewling and puking in her mother's arms. She might bump into him or her and never know. She remembers Joe's quest to meet his long lost Seela. Poor little Joe, now long lost himself. Such sweet good people all of them. Don't think about it, she tells herself, not for the first time, move on, forward. You will never knowingly see any of them again unless of course someone gets hold of Liddell's formula, which is unlikely as they seem to have stamped pretty efficiently on his Internet sites. She pats the bag of the last of the drugs she had rescued, enough for three more weeks. She has carried on working diligently on transferring the memories over the last year. Once she is speaking Xhosa every day that should gel nicely and she should need them no more.

She takes a sip of water from a large white polyester canister and feels a deep longing for a certain home-brewed alcoholic beverage that can give headaches of unbelievable pain. That may have to wait, it tends to be a male drink, certainly not for women of her age – anyway other familiar pleasures await; she starts the jeep again.

The track is getting very bumpy; she turns a corner and sees the village. It hits her like a blow. Not seen for thirty years but before that seen every day for a lifetime, a long and wonderful lifetime. She rolls the jeep to a halt and gets out. A trickle of curious villagers approach. Two or three children run up. She greets them in Xhosa and they answer unsurprised. Some adults also approach. A woman maybe ten years older than herself comes up – Costello says her name, and the woman is startled to be recognised by this strange white woman. Costello knows not to tell the woman she is her own (or is it his own) daughter and restrains the impulse to embrace her tightly. Maybe later, a lot later, a few years later. Quite a crowd is gathered now. Costello addresses them in Xhosa,

'Dear friends I would like to stay with you in your village.'

'For how long?' they ask.

'To stay for ever, to become part of you.'

A huddle of the more elderly villagers forms and they discuss the proposal. Eventually one turns to Costello,

'Does the jeep stay with you too?'

'Of course.'

'Then we agree. You will have to share a hut with this lady.'

An elderly woman is pushed forward. Costello knows her name but doesn't say it – not too much shock on the first day for these good people. She shakes the woman's hand with a stirring of some long remembered romantic involvement that came to nothing. Some of the children are in the cab of the jeep. One pushes the horn and startles herself.

She picks the child up and pops her by the side of the pickup.

'Bring out the canisters; we are going to fetch the water,' she orders them.

The children run and bring back a motley crowd of plastic and metal bottles and vessels which they pile in the back of the jeep before jumping on board themselves – three crowded into the cab the rest in the back.

'Do you know where the well is?' one of the villagers asks her.

Costello climbs up onto the driving seat, it is a bit of a squash.

'Know where it is? I dug it,' she says quietly to herself.

She sets off up the hill to a cheer from her passengers and the villagers stare after their new visitor who is at the same time strange but also strangely familiar.

Even once they can't see the small pickup anymore they can still hear shrill laughter and incessant tooting.